playing it
COOL

playing it
COOL

AMY
ANDREWS

Entangled Publishing, LLC
10940 S Parker Rd
Suite 327
Parker, CO 80134
rights@entangledpublishing.com

Brazen is an imprint of Entangled Publishing, LLC.

Edited by Liz Pelletier
Cover design by LJ Anderson/Mayhem Cover Creations
Cover photo by Lindee Robinson, featuring Matthew Engelke

Manufactured in the United States of America

First Edition September 2016

ENTANGLED
BRAZEN

To Curtis Svehlak from Entangled, for all the practical stuff you do behind the scenes.
We've never met but I feel like it's high time I said thanks to a guy who's in my inbox more than any other (and I mean that in a completely non-sleazy way).
I owe you a vat of whatever you're drinking when we do finally meet.

Chapter One

Dexter Blake liked a woman with some junk in her trunk. And the tall, curvy chick on the sidelines was packing a whole lot of booty. She had one of those itty-bitty waists, too. And her cups floweth'd over.

Staring at her chest was practically a religious experience.

Unfortunately, she only had eyes for Chuck Nugent, the pretty boy sports reporter for Channel Five. He was currently doing his sycophantish spiel on the field, a cameraman following him around as he interviewed the players still milling around for their obligatory post-match interviews.

She was impatient for his attention, too, if her pacing was anything to go by.

Lucky bastard.

As far as Dex was concerned, she could keep pacing. Watching everything jiggle was the cherry on the top of his pie tonight. There was nothing better than winning a hard-fought game of rugby union. But watching a fine-looking woman strutting her stuff came a very close second.

"I'd say don't look now, booty at six o'clock, but I can see you're ahead of me."

Dex smiled at Tanner Stone, the captain of the Sydney Smoke and his good mate, as he pulled up beside him then dropped at the waist to stretch out his hamstrings.

"I don't know what you're talking about."

"Hey, Dex," Bodie Webb said as he pulled up on the other side. "Your kinda ass on the sideline."

A low whistle came from behind them. "I hope you're planning on hitting that, Dex," Lincoln Quinn murmured as he also appeared, casually waving at some teenage girls hollering at him from the dispersing crowd.

Dex chuckled. "Since when did you all turn into pimps?"

Linc clapped him on the back. "Just lending a hand."

"Thanks. I can get my own ass."

And, sadly, as much as sideline-chick ticked every box, her ass was off-limits. One look at her told him she was the kind of girl a guy loved. Got into a relationship with. The kind he married. Made babies with.

She was the commitment type.

Over a decade of avoiding romantic entanglements had alerted Dex to the signs, and this woman had *I don't do casual* written all over her.

And he didn't do commitment. His career came first. He'd fought hard for his place on the team, and at thirty, he probably only had a few good years left. He couldn't afford to take his eyes off the ball for a second. He knew how easy it was to lose everything. To have it all go to shit when you least expected it.

He was never going back to Perry Hill.

There would be time for commitment later. Rugby was it for now.

"But you don't," Tanner said.

"Just because I don't walk around with a permanent hard-on like Linc—"

"Hey!"

Everyone ignored Linc's half-hearted protest. The cocky back rower wore his horniness like a badge of frickin' honour. "—doesn't mean I go without."

And if he did—it was none of their damn business.

Chuck finished his interview with the skipper of the losing team and, spotting Tanner, headed toward them.

"Christ," Dex said. "Dickhead approaching."

Tanner sighed. "Best to just think of our contracts and smile for the camera."

"Ooh, *hellllo*," Bodie purred. "She's on the move, too."

Dex's gaze flicked to the woman again, tracking her progress as she hurried after Chuck. Her hips swung enticingly and her chest moved interestingly beneath her T-shirt.

Christ, it was a turn-on.

"Chuck," she called, hurrying to catch up with him.

Idiot. Dex would never let a woman trail behind him like that. Not when she could walk in front and he could check out her luscious ass.

"What in hell does she see in that guy?" Bodie asked.

Dex had no idea, but the urge to throttle the smarmy reporter—something that was never far from the surface— spewed like the sudden rush of a geyser in his chest.

"Chuck," she called, louder this time, almost caught up with him.

Dickhead stopped. Turned. Then glared before looking around him as if he was embarrassed. He hissed, "What the fuck, Harper?" He'd kept his voice low, but the edge of fury carried it farther than Dex was sure Chuck would have liked.

"I told you to *stay* in the stands, not embarrass me by running onto the goddamn field in a pair of jeans you've barely managed to squeeze your lard ass into. I have a certain image to maintain, and it does not involve being followed around by fat chicks."

Dex's jaw clamped tight as the hackles rose on the back of his neck. *Fat chick?* He could see the stain of red creeping up her neck from here, and the spewing geyser in his chest turned viscous, like lava.

"God, he's a fuckwit," Bodie whispered.

"Excuse me," Dex growled.

Lava burning in his chest, he strode purposefully toward Chuck and the woman, who was hissing something back at the reporter Dex couldn't quite hear. He was sweaty and dirty and every damn muscle bitched at him, but Dex paid none of it any heed.

The urge to deck the smarmy front man rode him hard, but by the time he pulled up beside Chuck, Dex had another plan.

A better plan.

One that involved less potential penalty. And more potential booty.

"Hey, Chuck," he said, forcing himself to smile as he clapped the reporter hard on the back. It was satisfying to hear a strained, involuntary cough from the man.

"Oh Dex, hi," Chuck said, sleazy smile in place, turning as if he were trying to block the woman from Dex's view.

No chance with those puny coat hanger shoulders.

"Great game tonight," Chuck enthused. "If you could just give me thirty seconds, I'll be right over."

"Actually, Chuck," Dex glanced at the woman and smiled at her. She was even more magnificent up close, with a whole lot of pissed-off glittering in the depths of her Marsala brown eyes. "I was hoping you might introduce me to the lady."

It was amusing to watch the pretty boy almost choke on his tongue. For a moment, Dex thought he was going to say *lady, what lady?* But he finally turned to acknowledge the woman behind him. "Of course. This is Harper…Nugent. My…"

The woman—*Harper*—folded her arms across her chest, and all the blood rushed from Dex's big head to his little one. "Come on, Chuck, you can say it," she said, her voice dry with amused sarcasm. "It starts with S. *Ssss*ister."

Something eased in Dex's chest. So she was *not* getting naked with Pretty Boy. There was a God.

"Step!" Chuck said quickly, his voice sharp.

She rolled her eyes as she smiled at Dex and offered her hand. He absently noted there were streaks of paint on her fingers. "Nice to meet you."

Dex was a tall guy. Big. Not as big as some of the team's front row, but he was still six foot and had trouble buying shirts that weren't tight in the shoulders. This tall—hell, *Amazonian*—woman could look him straight in the eye. He'd never met a woman who could do that in a pair of flats, and it was a strange kind of turn-on.

"The pleasure's entirely mine," he murmured, returning her firm and sure grip with one of his own.

He liked a woman who could handshake like a boss.

"Yes…anyway," Chuck said, his expression pained, as Harper's hand fell away. "Harper has to run. A girlfriend crisis or something."

Dex's eyebrow kicked up. A girlfriend crisis? A crushing sense of disappointment slugged him in the chest.

She was a lesbian?

She laughed and shook her head. "Not *that k*ind of girlfriend."

His gaze was drawn to her mouth, a plush, sexy crescent in the midst of her flawless olive complexion. He didn't think she was wearing any makeup, but she was sporting some kind of clear lip gloss that emphasized the luscious curve of her lips.

They glistened, wet and tempting.

Dex laughed, too, as relief flowed like champagne bubbles

through his veins. "I am *so* pleased to hear that."

Chuck cleared his throat. "Yes. Well. I have to interview the team." He looked pointedly at his sister.

"Fine. Just don't forget to pick up Jace and Tabby after you're done. They're fine in the stands with Jenny while you wrap up, but she can't take them home and I've told your mother that you're bringing her kids now instead of me."

"I'm not going to bloody forget them, Harper," Chuck replied testily.

She shot an apologetic smile at Dex then turned to go. He and Chuck watched her. The outline of her sexy, rounded butt in the denim of her jeans actually made Dex a little light-headed. It was a sight to behold.

"God, she has a fat ass," Chuck muttered, disgust colouring his voice.

Dex's hands tightened to fists. *What a monumental wanker.* He opened his mouth before he engaged his brain. "Harper! Wait up."

She looked over her shoulder, a puzzled expression drawing a crease between her brows. "Dex," Chuck said, putting a hand on Dex's arm as he took a step in Harper's direction.

"Tanner's waiting," Dex said, shaking off the hand before jogging the short distance to where she'd stopped.

"Hey," she said, tossing the long strands of her rich dark hair behind her shoulder, clearly still puzzled.

He smiled. "I was hoping you might like to go out with me one night."

She blinked, the crease between her eyebrows almost cavernous now. "Oh."

Dex chuckled. It wasn't the standard response he got from women. Normally, they were tripping over themselves to be asked out by him. Hell, most of them didn't wait to be asked. It was well known that he didn't generally date, so they were more than happy to do the asking.

A man with a less healthy ego might have been insulted by Harper's tepid response. But he could sense her reticence was real as she glanced at the guys to her left, all gawking and smirking, clearly talking about them. Her gaze travelled over his shoulder to where Chuck stood—glaring, if the prickle between Dex's shoulder blades was anything to go by.

Her gaze returned to him. "Um…"

Hmm. Maybe this wasn't going to be as easy as he'd thought. He looked pointedly at the mobile she held. "Give me your phone."

She glanced at it for a moment, frowning some more. "Why?"

Dex gave an exaggerated sigh and plucked it out of her unresisting hand. "It's okay," he assured her as she murmured a protest, and his fingers busily navigating to her address book. "I'm just going to put my number in because obviously I don't have my phone available to put yours into mine."

She crossed her arms as she watched him enter the details, and it took him twice as long.

"There," he said, passing the phone back to her.

She glanced at the entry, and his heart tap-danced in his chest as a smile pulled at the curve of her mouth. She quirked an eyebrow at him. "Dex the Stud?"

He grinned and shrugged. "What can I say?"

"And what do you expect me to do with this?"

"As soon as you're done with your girlfriend thing, give it a ring and we can set up a time and a place for our date."

"Well, that's a step up from the last guy, who put his number into my phone hoping I'd send him nude photos," she said, her tone flippant.

Dex blinked. *What the actual fuck?* "Absolutely no class."

"Well, to be fair, he did request *arty* ones."

He laughed. "Hey." He held his hands up in faux

surrender. "Never let it be said that I stand in the way of artistic expression, if you feel so inclined with my number. But definitely lose his."

She laughed back, and it grabbed him by the balls. Like everything else about her, it was big and rich and real. But then her gaze flicked over his shoulder again, and her smile slowly slipped from her face.

Dex gave an exaggerated sigh. "You're not going to ring it, are you?"

She shook her head, a glossy smile playing on her glossy mouth. "No chance in hell."

"Why?"

She glanced at her stepbrother again. "Some things just aren't worth the hassle."

Dex couldn't agree more. But he didn't think Harper Nugent was one of them. Undeterred, he grabbed for her phone again, his reflexes lightning fast after a decade of professional rugby. "You leave me no choice," he chided as he quickly rang his own number.

"Hi, Dex the Stud," he said as the ring tone eventually gave way to his message bank. "It's Dex." He waggled his brows at Harper, and she smiled and rolled her eyes. "I'm ringing to remind you to call Harper Nugent on this number and ask her on a date again. Do not take no for an answer. Even"—he grinned at her—"if she offers nude arty photos in lieu."

Dex hit the end button and passed the phone back to her. "There now. You're in my phone. And I *will* be ringing you."

She glanced at the phone then at him before flicking a look at the guys again. Linc was grinning like a loon as he shot Dex two thumbs-up.

"Sure you will," she said, the tight, polite smile on her face making Dex want to slap Linc upside the head.

She bade him farewell and walked away, and for the first

time in his life, Dex looked forward to something other than rugby and inflicting bodily harm on Linc.

• • •

Harper's phone rang three hours later. She was a bottle of wine down with her best friend Em, who was in the middle of a boyfriend-number-sixteen crisis. Em was cute, peppy, and up for anything.

She just had really lousy taste in men.

When Em went into a relationship, she went all in, something which Harper had always admired even if her friend consistently chose the wrong guys to be "in" with. The type who were only out for a *good* time, not a *long* time. But she always sprang back, and Harper was in awe of her friend's tenacity and absolute conviction that the right person was out there for everyone.

Although not tonight. While Harper was drinking wine, Em's breakup booze of choice was butterscotch schnapps, and tonight it was leading her to seriously consider becoming a nun. To prove her seriousness, she was currently Googling how to re-virginise.

So, Harper was both tipsy and completely distracted when she answered the phone.

"Hi," she said as Em made gagging noises at pictures on a website she was skimming.

"Hey, Harper."

The hairs on the back of her neck stood up in instant awareness as they had earlier tonight when Dexter Blake had singled her out for a bit of attention.

Her mind went blank for a beat or two. *He rang?*

Of course he had. She had clearly been some kind of bet or dare or something with his team buddies. At twenty-three, it wouldn't be the first time she'd been the butt of some douche's idea of a good time. *I dare you to ask the fat chick out.* Snigger, snort, backslap.

Some men were such assholes.

But it had been *so* good, even momentarily, to put her sanctimonious step-brother in his place.

"Harper? It's Dex the Stud. Remember me?"

His voice was warm and rich with amusement, and Harper shut her eyes. *Remember him?* She'd relived him asking her out about a dozen times, no matter how much she'd told herself it had all been some sick joke. It had been the first thing she'd told Em after her friend had stopped crying and asked for something happy to cheer her up.

Then they'd Googled him.

"Harper?"

His voice was sharper this time and Harper pulled herself together, sitting straighter in the chair. "Yes. Of course… Hi."

"You sound kinda…outta it."

Harper eyed the empty wine bottle and the full one she'd just cracked open. "Well…I'm kinda drunk, so that's probably why."

His low chuckle slid seductive fingers down her neck. "The girlfriend emergency?"

"Yup."

Em looked over her shoulder. "Who is it?"

"Dex."

Her eyebrows practically hit her hairline. "The rugby dude?"

"Is that the girlfriend?" Dex asked in her ear.

"Yup," she said to them both.

"Ask him if he knows how to re-virginise."

Harper shook her head. "I'm not asking him that."

"Asking me what?" His voice sounded delicious when it was amused. Thick and gooey, oozing all over her body. Like chocolate topping.

God, she loved chocolate topping.

"You should totally ask me whatever it is."

"Trust me, you don't want to know."

"Are you kidding?" Em interrupted. "He's a professional rugby star. Everyone knows they get laid all the time. What he doesn't know about a woman's anatomy probably isn't worth knowing. He'll know about re-virginising."

Harper thought it more likely he'd know about *de-*virginising.

"Did she just say re-virginising?"

Had Harper been sober, she would have paid more heed to Em's sage words about the mating habits of professional sportsmen and not the sweet seduction of a chocolate-topping voice. She sighed. "Yup."

"Why would anyone want to re-virginise? Hell... *Can* someone re-virginise?"

"I don't know and yes, apparently, according to the internet. Spiritually and surgically."

"That sounds...painful."

Harper laughed. "Yes. For both."

"And seriously, would you want some strange dude with a scalpel down near your lady parts?"

She shuddered. "I can think of better uses for a dude down near my lady parts." His bark of laughter was loud in her ear, and she realised what she said. Her face flamed. "Oh God, sorry. I said that out loud, didn't I?"

"You certainly did, Harper Nugent."

"I take it back."

"Oh no," he chuckled some more. "You can't take *that* back."

Harper groaned internally. *Jesus.* Where was her filter? She glanced at the wine bottle. Somewhere at the bottom of that, no doubt.

"Fine. Ignore it then. It's the booze. White wine makes

me mouthy."

"I can't wait to see that."

His voice had dropped an octave and roughened with the merest hint of a promise. It went straight to those aforementioned lady parts, and Harper actually squirmed in her chair to ease the sudden ache.

"She's not serious, is she?"

It took her a moment to realise he'd moved on, and she leaped at the opportunity gratefully. "No. She's pissed. Both at men and in the alcoholic sense." Em had already been several shots of Schnapps down when Harper arrived. "Re-virginising is just one of many options we've already discussed tonight. I think she wants to make a voodoo doll next."

He laughed again. "I like the sound of her."

Harper sighed, looking at the gorgeous mop of caramel curls and the alabaster wedge of cheekbone making up Em's profile. She looked like one of those babies from old-fashioned adverts for Pears soap. Only all grown-up.

"She's gorgeous. You should ask *her* out. You'd make beautiful babies."

There was a long pause. Long enough to make Harper think, somewhere in her alcohol-addled brain, babies were not on Dexter Blake's agenda.

"Thanks," he said, voice low and amused. "I think I'll stick with my original plan, though."

"Oh?"

"You and me. A date."

"Oh." Harper's stomach tightened. She'd seen the way his teammates had been watching them tonight. The way the younger guy had given the thumbs up. She could have kissed Dex for his timing, but a girl had her pride, right? Plus she never wanted to be one of *those* people who were gossiped about for *punching above her weight*.

"Look. I'm very flattered that you want to go out on a

date with me, but—"

"You should do it," Em interrupted.

Harper blinked at her best friend. "What?"

"I told you I liked the sound of her," Dex said in her ear.

Em shrugged. "It'd be worth it just to piss off Chuckers." If it was possible, Em disliked Chuck more than Harper did.

Harper considered that angle for moment, her head still spinning a little. It was a powerful argument. Why not? If Dex was using her to win some kind of ridiculous frat boy dare, why shouldn't she use him, too?

"Okay, fine." Clearly there was a level of drunk where pride rapidly diminished. "But I'm not sleeping with you. Or letting you anywhere near my lady parts."

That low chuckle again. It ruffled seductively along flesh and nerve endings, and Harper fought the urge to stretch. And purr.

"You know you said that out loud, too, right?"

The lazy smile in his voice ruffled things even lower. "Yes. I know."

"I will be on my best behaviour. I promise I won't even bring condoms."

Sober Harper nodded, pleased with the concession. Drunk, uninhibited Harper knew full well he could ruin her without the aid of a condom, and she seemed perfectly fine with that, too.

Uninhibited Harper was dangerous. She was going to have to cut that bitch off at the knees.

Chapter Two

The following Wednesday night, Harper sat at a paint-splattered table, tapping her paint-stained fingers.

Dex was ten minutes late.

Or not coming. Which was probably more likely.

Maybe he only had to score a date, not actually go through with it, to win the bet? Maybe he'd had a better offer from one of the many skinny women he'd been photographed with?

Harper's obsessive Googling had not been good for her ego.

The women seemed to fall into two categories—female footy fans at matches, in their Smoke jerseys and scarves, clinging to his sweaty, postgame arms, or glamorous creatures in evening gowns, his arm around *them* as they posed for the media on red carpets.

Now she wished she'd stayed well away from the internet, because clearly she wasn't his type at all. Neither the skinny type, nor the clingy type. As Chuck had been at pains to point out when he'd found out about the date and rang to express his displeasure.

Thankfully it had gone to her voice mail.

Guys like Dexter Blake don't get involved with big *women when they can have supermodels.* And then he'd finished it with a plea to think about his career. *For God's sake, don't eat in front of him or do anything desperate to embarrass me or my standing with the studio.*

God, he was *such* a tosser, and it felt good to be doing something to piss him off. Hell, if it wasn't for Jace and Tabby, she'd have nothing at all to do with him or his mother and their toxic worship of the superficial.

Harper glanced at her watch. Fifteen minutes. Was it too early to feel stood up? But then her mobile chimed, and a rush of relief flowed through her as she spied the message from Dex.

Ack! Sorry. Traffic awful. Am five away. Please don't leave. Have been looking forward to this all week.

Harper smiled despite all her reservations. If he was using her, he was being respectful about it. She tapped out her response.

Not leaving. Drinking wine. Be afraid. Be very afraid.

She took another sip of wine, conscious that it was half gone already and she needed to be sober around him in case she blurted out something else about her lady parts. Like how it'd been his face she'd pictured the last four nights when she'd brought her vibrator out to play.

He rushed in five minutes later. "I'm sorry," he apologised, pulling up the chair opposite. "Training ran late. Griff had a bug up his ass about something. Then the traffic."

Harper noted the lack of criticism in Dex's voice regarding his coach. It was more matter-of-fact, like it was a common occurrence and neither here nor there. Griffin King, rugby union's most successful coach, was known for being a tough taskmaster.

She'd Googled that, too.

"It's fine." She smiled at him, her heart tripping at the damp curl of his hair at his collar and the shadow of whiskers on his jaw. She wondered what they'd feel like scraping down her belly, and squeezed her thighs together tightly as muscles deep and low responded to the image. Honestly, it was like a tap had been loosened down there, and with every wicked thought—and they were frequent—things got wetter.

She held up her glass. "I had company."

He grinned. "Does this mean you're going to get mouthy?"

His gaze dropped to her lips, and Harper battled the urge to lick them nervously. "I hate to disappoint you, but it takes more than half a glass."

And telling Dexter Blake she was so horny for him she'd worn out a set of batteries was something she planned on taking to her grave.

"Well then," he murmured, light green eyes suddenly twinkling with mischief, "let's get you a top-up."

Harper smiled as he gestured to the waiter. Her gaze shifted to the way his button-down shirt strained at his shoulders. It drifted lower to the dark hair covering strong forearms.

Strong enough to hold her.

She squeezed her thighs tighter, wishing she hadn't worn jeans as the middle seam pressed torturously good against aching flesh.

The waiter recognised Dex and asked if he could have a selfie with him. Dex politely declined, joking good-naturedly to give Dex a break because he was trying to impress a girl. The waiter took it well, leaving a drink and tapas menu and promising to be right back, but Harper could tell that the exchange had bothered Dex.

She looked around the three-quarters full art bar, noticing the sidelong glances as people realised they had a *star* in their midst. "Does that happen often?"

"Often enough." His tone was clipped.

"You don't like it?"

"I don't mind it when I'm at a game or doing something official for rugby." He shrugged. "It's part of the territory. But when I'm out as a private citizen?" He shook his head. "Well…let's just say I tend to avoid it as much as possible."

Harper frowned. "Avoid being recognised?"

"Avoid going out."

Except he did go out. She'd seen him on her computer screen looking tall and dark and dashing in his tuxedo, walking the red carpet with glamorous women draped on his arm. Or was that official rugby business, too?

"We don't have to stay," she said. "We can go someplace quieter and out of the way, if you like?"

She'd chosen The Art Bar, a trendy new wine and paint bar, because it was casual and relaxed and she knew the owners. She'd come several times with friends. Painting their own masterpieces as they drank booze and nibbled from the tapas menu made for a fun night out, and the activity took the pressure off for conversation, the perfect way to circumvent any awkward silences.

"No, its fine." He shook his head instantly and smiled, and she felt like he really wanted to be here. "I can't even draw a stick figure, but I'm game if you are. How does it work?"

Harper explained the rules. She told him there'd be a theme, and an hour to paint, then talked about her friends Brianne and Kevin, who'd started the business six months ago, and what a runaway success it had been. She talked until their first plate of tapas arrived—mouth-watering, piping-hot spring rolls—and two blank one-foot-square canvases, complete with miniature easel and paint-pot stands, had been delivered to all the tables.

"Tonight's theme is 'lush,'" Kevin announced. Most of the

tables in the restaurant had at least eight people, some even more, and there were good-natured groans from the different groups. But there was much excitement, too, a low buzz circulating quickly as the participants discussed the theme.

"That's kind of a broad topic," Dex said.

Harper grinned. "That's the point. It gives you a lot of scope. You know what you're going to paint?"

His gaze dropped to her mouth and fanned over her chest. Her modest shirt was buttoned high, revealing no discernible cleavage, but she suddenly felt naked under the intensity of his stare.

Her nipples hardened to two tight points, and she was glad for the looseness of her blouse and grateful they were at a table for two.

"Oh yeah." He lifted his beer bottle to his lips and took a long swallow. His neck moved convulsively, and Harper was hyperaware of his stubbly throat, of the thud of his pulse in his neck. "You?"

Currently the lush bound of his carotid was looking pretty damn good. "Um yes," she said faintly, turning her attention to the canvas and dipping her paintbrush in the green pot, quickly outlining a leaf. And then another.

Rainforests were lush, right?

She was relieved when he dabbed a paintbrush into the red pot and started painting on his canvas, his head to one side.

He used long, sweeping strokes as she watched him surreptitiously through her fringe. They were quite hypnotic. And sexy. She'd fantasised about him using long, sweeping strokes on himself, making himself come at her command as the fantasy reached fever pitch and she'd increased the speed on her vibrator.

Muscles behind her belly button contracted, clamping down hard at the thought. Who'd have thought long, slow strokes could be such a freaking turn-on?

"So, Harper Nugent," he said after a minute or two. "What is it you do for a living?"

Harper startled at the unexpected conversation. He stopped the long strokes as he waited for her to reply, and the tight clench of her body gave way in one reflexive shudder.

She'd had orgasms that hadn't been as good.

Her breath eased slowly from her body, and she cleared her throat as she shifted against the stool to relieve the hard ache between her legs. "I'm an artist."

He narrowed his eyes. "What kind of an artist?"

"A painter...a muralist to be precise. For the moment, anyway."

"Ah." His gaze flicked to her hands, already stained with paint. "That explains that then."

Harper's glance followed his. No doubt he was used to women with much more glamorous hands. Soft skin, elegant fingers, long, glossy, painted nails. Her hands were dry and rough. With hands in paint and solvents all bloody day, Harper's skin was more crocodile than human. Her cuticles and nail beds were stained with the marks from her latest commission.

"So..." he continued, a low teasing note in his voice, "choosing this place was to get the rugby player out of his comfort zone, huh? I'm over here finger painting and you're creating something Picasso would be proud of."

His grin was crooked and charming and Harper couldn't help but grin in return. "It's not a competition."

"*Everything's* a competition, Harper."

He was smiling, but there was a seriousness to his voice. How else *would* an elite athlete think?

"You can't win all the time." Winning at freakish, orgasmic mind control over her body was more than enough for one night, surely? "But for damn sure I'm going to kick your ass tonight."

He hooted out a surprised laugh. "I knew there was a competitive streak inside you."

Harper shrugged. "If it's any consolation, I'd suck at rugby." Although God knew, she could hack being *rucked* by Dexter Blake.

He looked her over appreciatively. Like he was thinking the *exact* same thing. "It's like anything else. You just need to practise."

She quirked an eyebrow. "Like art?"

He flicked a glance at his canvas and grimaced. "Touché."

The waiter arrived with the next two tapas plates and the moment was lost. He offered her some divine smelling flash-fried calamari and some Haloumi drenched in lemon juice and garnished with rock salt and a sprig of rocket.

She declined.

"You've barely eaten anything," he protested.

Harper shrugged. "I'm not hungry." It was a bald-faced lie but bloody Chuck had made her so self-conscious about eating in front of Dex that she couldn't do it, not even to spite him. She just hoped her growling stomach didn't get any louder.

"You eat it," she insisted. "You look like you need constant feeding and watering just to fulfill basic functions."

He speared a succulent piece of calamari with his fork, his gaze locking with hers. "A person needs more than food and water."

Her own needs reared to the surface as a smear of oil and some crumbs coated the corner of his mouth. The urge to lick them off drummed in her chest as real as her own heartbeat.

"Yeah, well," she said, breaking their eye contact to inspect the progress of her painting. Already little forest creatures were taking shape, peeping out from behind the lush green leaves. "Food is all that's on offer here tonight, buddy."

And maybe if she told herself that often enough, she'd quash the wicked whispers from uninhibited Harper, who seemed to have escaped the straitjacket she'd been restrained in since their phone call the other night.

Harper—the uninhibited *and* sober versions—didn't have a problem with one-night stands. She didn't give a rat's ass what two consenting adults decided—more power to them. She just didn't believe in it for herself. Sleeping with a guy—any guy—on the first date was not on her agenda. And even if she were to break that lifelong rule, she sure as hell wasn't going to head down that path with a guy she knew was using her as much as she was using him.

What if she wanted more, but he and his mates had had their fun and he moved on? To a *supermodel*. That was just asking for some fucked-up self-doubt that would screw with her psyche for far too long.

"And painting," she added. "Take it or leave it."

A smile played on the full curve of his bottom lip as he considered her for a moment. Weighing his options maybe? God knew she was so turned on from watching his wrist action he could slide his hand onto her thigh and she'd probably come louder than Sally had done for Harry.

And there'd be nothing fake about it.

Harper almost sagged with relief in her chair when he picked up his paintbrush and dipped it in the white paintpot before transferring it to his canvas, resuming the incessant long, slow strokes.

"Do you have a current commission you're working on?" he asked after a moment or two.

"Yup," she said, also returning her attention to her own work. "I'm currently doing murals for the City Central kid's hospital."

"Really?" His eyebrows rose in interest. "The club does charity stuff there. We've got a visit coming up soon, I think. How'd that gig come about?"

"A friend of mine has a child with cystic fibrosis who's in

and out of there a lot. The place was so bloody depressing—all the walls this beigey-apricot colour. Looked like it was the original paint job from two decades prior. She raised some funds and got permission to have murals painted on the walls of the ward where Maddy stays, to brighten things up a bit and make the kids less apprehensive about being in some giant, sterile, unfriendly building. She suggested me for the murals. I put some designs together and was given the go ahead."

He whistled, clearly impressed. "That sounds awesome."

The enthusiasm in his voice was genuine, and Harper sat a little higher. She'd been so used to her so-called family nagging her about getting a proper job, she'd forgotten that there was another worldview out there. "I *do* have an awesome job." She grinned.

"How long have you been doing this?"

"The first ward was a year ago, but I'm doing various wings in the entire hospital now. I also volunteer to teach a couple of art classes through the school there in the afternoons."

"They have a school?"

"Sure. Some kids are long-term, and they have as much right to be educated as well kids."

"Makes sense," he mused. "So…you're a muralist by trade?"

"No. I'm a graphic artist, which is useful in the design stage. But I know my way around a canvas, too, and just sort of fell into this, and I love it."

"That is so cool. Your family must be really proud."

Harper kept her smile in place but it was tight and forced. "I think they'd prefer me to have a *real* job."

He frowned. "Being an artist isn't a real job?

"Well…" She shrugged. "To be fair, it's not always stable and usually not very lucrative."

"And is that the way we measure job worth? By how lucrative it is?"

Harper gave a half laugh. "It's the way a lot of people do."

"We're talking about Chuck now, right?"

"My stepbrother..." Harper picked her way carefully through this. She didn't have a lot of time for Chuck—she certainly didn't feel like she owed him any family loyalty—but he did have to work with guys like Dex, and she had no desire to fuck anything up for him, either. "Let's just say we don't see eye to eye."

"How in the hell did you come to have the misfortune of being related to that tosser?"

Harper blinked at the patent distaste in Dex's voice. "He's not...liked?"

According to Chuck—who had the good fortune to be born with classic, clean-cut good looks and a great physique—he was Mr. Popularity. Apparently all the footy players loved him and, with his unparalleled ratings, he was being groomed to host the studio's rugby show when the position next became vacant.

Her gaze roamed over Dexter Blake's face. He wasn't classically good-looking at all. Sure, he was tall and broad, but his dark hair was a little too unruly and there was nothing clean-cut about the rugged, stomped-on features that gave him the rather battered appearance worn by a lot of rugby players.

But his face did more for her than Chuck's brand of pretty ever had.

"Not liked?" He laughed and it was music to Harper's ears. "He's barely tolerated. He's a total dick who cares more about looking good and getting his face on the camera than he does any hard-hitting sports news. But hey...the female audiences love him." His brow scrunched, accentuating the rugged appearance. "Apparently."

The last was said with such confusion that Harper laughed. "It's okay. I don't get it, either."

She'd seen too much of his ugly heart to consider him any kind of attractive.

"Have you been related long?"

Harper doodled paint absently on her canvas, not really paying too much attention to what she was creating, the paintbrush as much an extension of her as a ball was to Dex. She sipped her wine, trying to decide whether she should go into all the gory details. Ultimately, with Dex's long, slow strokes distracting her, she found herself wanting to tell him.

"I was ten when my dad married Chuck's mother. He was fourteen. And well and truly the golden boy as far as my stepmum Anthea is concerned."

"So he was always a prick?"

Harper's mouth lifted in a wry smile. "Pretty much. I think he was threatened that I was as tall as him and not some pretty, dainty little girl who was going to hero worship him. He used to call me harpoon because that's what whales like me needed."

Dex's hand stilled mid-stroke and his knuckles turned white. "Did you tell your dad?"

"Nah." Harper had been lucky to have Em and a decade of body-positive messages that had given her a good sense of herself, even if the crushing weight of a society obsessed with bodily perfection played havoc with her confidence from time to time. "He was happy after being sad for so long about Mum dying. And Anthea was okay. I mean…she was cute and petite and blonde and ate like a sparrow, and I think my size eleven shoes were a constant embarrassment to her, but it wasn't really until after my dad died a few years ago that it's become all about Chuck again. Especially since his big nomination for the annual television awards. Anyone would think he was up for a freaking Nobel Prize."

"So…if your dad's not around anymore, why have anything to do with Chuck and his mother at all?" he asked, dipping his paintbrush in the red again.

"Because when I was twelve they had twins—Jace and Tabby. They're my brother and sister and they mean the world to me. When Dad died, they were the same age I was when I'd lost my mother to a car accident, and I promised my father while he was in the hospital that I would always look out for them. So I grit my teeth and pretend all is peachy."

"You stay involved with them?"

Harper nodded. "My stepmother works full time as an interior designer, and with my job being flexible, I do the school pick up and run them around to their different activities in the afternoon until Anthea gets home. They often come and stay with me on the weekends."

He painted for a beat or two, his gaze fixed on the canvas. "I'm sorry about your father."

"Thanks." Harper gave him a sad smile.

He glanced at her and returned the expression with one of his own, as if he knew a little about grief, too. The chime of an incoming text broke the fledgling intimacy.

"Sorry," Harper grimaced, putting her wineglass down to pick up her phone.

Normally she wouldn't look at her phone on a date—even a fake one, but Harper was waiting on a reply from Tabby who hadn't been feeling well.

Alas, it was from Anthea...

Harper! Chuck just told me about this ridiculous pity date. It's probably just some kind of dare. I hope you're not embarrassing Chuck by throwing yourself at Dexter Blake. Set your sights lower and have more self-respect!

Harper was well used to Anthea being Chuck's mouthpiece by now. But considering how much she did for her stepmother, and how much she put up with from her, this level of vitriol really hurt.

Okay, yes, the date was fake, but was it really *that* ridiculous that a man of Dexter's calibre might want to go out with her?

Harper clutched the phone hard as she stared at the screen, her heart banging against her ribs as the words burrowed like a parasite under her skin. She was beginning to feel like a character in a fairy tale. The bad pantomime version.

Wicked stepmother, shitty stepbrother, poor, downtrodden orphan girl.

And it really wasn't that bad, for crying out loud. Anthea just didn't understand the value of a good heart over a good body. She'd been raised by an ex-beauty-queen mother and a mostly absent father who'd run a modelling agency. If she'd been someone else's stepmother, Harper might even have felt sorry for her.

But she wasn't.

A sudden yearning for her father swelled in her chest, and an unexpected rush of hot tears pricked the backs of her eyes.

"Is everything okay?"

Harper blinked furiously to quash the rise of tears. "Ah... sure," she said, putting the phone on the table with fingers that trembled slightly. She plastered a smile on her face as she grappled to bring her emotions under control.

The last thing she wanted to do was burst into tears in front of Dex. She wasn't sure how well rugby front-rowers coped with hysterical dates.

"Harper!" The call from across the room came at just the right moment. "Over here." Kevin gestured for her to join him. "You've just got to see this painting."

Harper leaped at the opportunity for escape. A chance to pull herself together. To remove herself from the heavy weight of Dex's concerned gaze.

She scraped her chair back, grateful beyond belief. "Won't be a moment," she said and fled to the other side of the room.

Chapter Three

Dex blinked at the retreating back of Harper Nugent. What the hell was that? Everything had been fine, and then her olive complexion had turned to alabaster as she read a text. Then she'd looked at him with moisture turning her eyes into deep Marsala pools.

He had absolutely no qualms reaching for her discarded phone and reading the text that was still on the screen. It was so awful he had to read it twice.

What the fuck?

Her *stepmother* had sent her this? No wonder Chuck was such a prick—it was obviously genetic.

Set her sights lower? Embarrassing *Chuck*? Probably some kind of dare?

Dare? What the fuck did she mean by that?

Dex dropped the phone, shuddering at the vileness, the rage he'd felt on the field the other night at hearing the way Chuck had talked to his sister returning. Harper was funny and witty and kind—being there to commiserate with her bestie, looking out for her siblings, volunteering her time at the hospital—any guy would be lucky to be with her.

And that didn't even go anywhere near her physical attributes. The strength of her Amazonian body, curves that wouldn't quit, an ass that he couldn't wait to get his hands on, and her mouth… Man, that mouth, all full and glistening with gloss again tonight.

Lush.

He glanced at his painting—a hopelessly inadequate 2D representation. The fullness didn't do it justice. The wetness wasn't right. The contours of her lips were not as perfectly defined. Her mouth was a goddamn frickin' work of art. How did he even capture that?

More importantly, how in hell was she even still single?

He glanced back toward Harper to find her making her way to the table, a really full glass of wine in her hand. Her jeans clung lovingly to her thighs and hips, and her hair, pulled back into a ponytail, swished behind her. Things moved interestingly under her shirt.

"Sorry 'bout that," she chirped, an overly bright smile fixed on her face as she sat. "Did you want another drink? I can call the waiter."

Dex shook his head. He only ever sat on one drink when he was out in public. Too many footy players got themselves into trouble by overindulging and acting like dicks.

"No, thanks."

"You should see some of the other paintings," she continued, still bright as a button. "I'm always amazed at people's creativity."

Dex picked up her phone. He sure as hell wasn't going to sit here and pretend like nothing had happened or let the vile insinuations of the message go uncountered. "I read your text."

Her chest puffed up, and for a moment he thought she was going to tell him off for invading her privacy, and to mind his own goddamn business. Both of which he deserved. Instead her shoulders slumped, her smile faded, and she stared morosely into her wine.

"It's fine." She dismissed the matter with a shrug. "Don't worry about it."

Don't worry about it? Was she crazy? "This date is not some dare."

The contortion of disbelief on her face was comical. "Oh, come on, Dex," she said briskly, her look incredulous. "I saw all your little rugby mates laughing and talking about us and shooting you the thumbs up the other night. It's okay. I understand how these things go. I was using you, too, to get up Chuck's nose. So we're even."

"No. You're wrong," he said as she took two decent gulps of her wine. "Nobody *dared* me to ask you on a date."

"Okay, sure," she said. "Maybe they bet you instead. Whatever. There's no need to get hung up on the semantics."

"Nope." Dex put his hand on his heart. "Absolutely not. No bet."

She waved her hand as if it was of no consequence. "So why are we here, then?" she insisted.

"I heard the way Chuck was talking to you at the game the other night, and I couldn't stand it."

She stared at him for long moments then laughed suddenly, a slight note of disbelief in the sound. "Oh God. I *am* in a pantomime, and you're the dashing prince sweeping in to rescue me from my evil stepbrother."

"Okay, sure. I can be the dashing prince." He grinned. "I can be whatever you want."

She didn't seem impressed by his offer. "So I *am* a pity date. Score one for Anthea."

Dex shuddered. No way in hell was that bitch going to score any points on his watch. "*No*. Trust me, I'd been lusting after you on the sidelines long before that."

She cocked an eyebrow at him, clearly disbelieving. "So you were going to ask me out, anyway?"

Dex hesitated. The urge to be honest warring with his need to protect her feelings.

Ultimately, honesty won out.

"No."

"Yeah." She nodded triumphantly. "That's what I thought."

"It's not like that." Dex reached across the table and slid his hand onto her forearm. "Look…" He sighed. Where to start? "I don't usually date, all right?"

She snorted. "Not according to the internet."

He grimaced. He knew the kind of photos that floated around the web. Selfies snapped by female fans at matches, and the official engagements and award ceremonies he attended as part of his commitments—contractual and social—to the Sydney Smoke.

"I haven't dated any of those women. That just goes with the rugby territory. Official crap."

"Oh, I don't know," she said, taking another long swallow of her wine, displacing his hand in the process. "I saw a couple of very non-official looking ones, too."

Dex laughed. "Those aren't me. In *any* way, shape, or form." He knew about them, though. His head Photoshopped onto some porn star's body, a twelve-inch schlong ready for action with some busty babe on her knees in front of him.

Dex wasn't exactly small in the junk department, but he didn't want to falsely advertise, either.

She eyed him for long moments, as if she were disappointed. "So *why* don't you date?"

"Because rugby is my number one priority at the moment. I had to fight hard to play professionally—I was overlooked a lot in my early career."

Dex had no desire to bring the mood down again by

talking about how difficult it was to pull himself free of the circumstances of his youth and prove himself a worthy contender. He didn't want her to think he was in it for the money, either, even if the thought of being on the bones of his ass again was highly motivating.

"But I'm here now, and at thirty I've probably only got another few years left in me, playing at an elite level, and relationships are distracting."

"But plenty of guys do it. Get married. Have families."

"Sure. It works for them. Me?" Dex shook his head. He'd been passed over for selection too often. "I worked too hard to get into the team, and there's such a narrow career window in professional sports, it *has* to be my focus. There'll be time for relationships later."

She tipped her head, considering him for a second. "Are you gay?"

Dex chuckled. "No." And if he *hadn't* been 100 percent sure about it before, then the rounded perfection of Harper's ass had confirmed it.

"So you're just…celibate?"

She sounded horrified, and he grinned. "Mostly. Occasionally I hook up but…" He shrugged. Having been caught out by one or two clingy women early in his career, Dex had learned to be careful.

"So you either have a really low sex drive, which is kinda surprising given the amount of testosterone you guys must pump out, or you…spend a *lot* of time in the shower."

The comment surprised a laugh out of Dex. He glanced at her wine—this was her third glass and she was half done with it. "Ah. Now we're getting to the mouthy bit."

"Have I shocked you?"

"Not at all. It's just that…and this may be because I don't chit-chat with a lot of women…masturbation isn't a topic I usually discuss with them."

"Why not? You discuss it with the guys, right?"

Dex shifted uncomfortably in his seat. All this talk about wanking was having a predictable effect. "Well, we might smack talk about it, but we don't sit around in the locker room having a serious discussion about how many times we did it the night before."

She quirked an eyebrow. "How *many* times?"

Heat rose in Dex's cheeks as he thought about how often in the last few days he'd tugged one off thinking about Harper. *Christ.* He'd been like a horny teenager all over again.

"Why, Dexter Blake, I do believe you're blushing. For a man who unashamedly read one of my private texts, I think it's a little late to come over all prudish now!"

She was grinning at him, obviously enjoying herself, and he relaxed. As far as Dex was concerned, it was a vast improvement on the shimmer of tears that goddamn text had caused.

And two could play at that game. Clearly they'd both given up on the whole painting lark.

He held up his hands in surrender. "Hey, you want to talk masturbation? I'm up for that. But you're talking to an expert here."

Her lips quirked, dragging his gaze south to their full, glossy pillows. "Expert, huh?"

"A Jedi," he deadpanned.

She laughed, but it was husky, the sound going straight to his balls. "A Jedi?"

He nodded. "Obi-*frickin*-wan, baby."

"What makes you think I'm not an expert?"

Dex tried *really* hard not to think about Harper lying gloriously naked on a bed touching herself. He failed. His cock surged to life, enjoying the visual.

"After all," she continued, winking at him. "I get to use props."

Another visual exploded into his brain. Harper gloriously naked on a bed touching herself, a light-sabre shaped dildo jammed to the hilt inside her.

Christ. He *really* liked her mouthy.

Ignoring the image, he pressed on. "Experts practise every day. When was the last time you did it?"

"Last night," she said, firing her response without even blinking. "You?"

He smiled triumphantly. "This morning. What do you think about when you touch yourself?"

"Lately?"

No. Every single time. God, he wanted every single dirty detail. But if she was the expert she professed, then that could take a while. He shrugged. "Sure."

"You."

Bam! Dex's cock almost burst through his zipper. She might as well have leaned over and shoved her hands down his pants.

She'd been fantasizing about *him* when she touched herself.

She grinned then like she knew *exactly* the affect that little bombshell had on him. "What about you, Dex?" she purred. "What's in your spank bank?"

"Lately?" he mimicked.

"Sure," she parried.

"Your ass."

She frowned, looking unsure of herself for the first time. "My…ass?"

"Oh yeah," he murmured, his dick twitching. "You have a *spectacular* ass."

She frowned as if the statement had genuinely confused her. "*My* ass?"

Dex grinned at her lack of understand. "*Your* ass. I think I've developed a completely unnatural obsession with it."

"Oh…" Light finally dawned in her eyes. "You're one of *those* guys."

"Those guys?"

"All about the bass."

"I am," Dex chuckled. "I really am."

"I've heard about your sort but thought you were just some kind of mythical beast. Like a unicorn."

Dex wondered if maybe he should be affronted by being compared to such a girly creature. He'd have preferred dragon. "Oh, we're real baby. Give me a woman with hips and boobs, thighs you can crack nuts with and an ass I can grab hold of, and I am a happy man."

"Hmm, that's funny," she murmured, dropping her head to the side a little as she inspected him. "None of those women I saw you pictured with seemed to fulfill *any* of that criteria."

He waved a dismissive hand. "They're normally just chicks the WAGS are trying to set me up with."

"So you're using them?"

"No. They're usually using *me*."

Dex could say that with absolute conviction. He was polite and gentlemanly. Hell, he was *charming*. He showed them a good time, and they were more than happy to have their selfies to take to work on Monday morning, or to post to their Facebook pages and imply a hell of a lot more than what had really happened with Dexter Blake, Sydney Smoke front-rower.

Dex didn't mind. It was all part of the unspoken deal. They had a splash of celebrity, and he got to keep his focus.

"And you haven't slept with *any* of them?"

He shook his head. As far as he was concerned, they'd all been very nice, but he'd only ever looked at them as props. A plus-one to an event he had to attend. Dex could put his hand on his heart and tell Harper with complete honesty that he'd never crossed that line.

Even though many had tried.

"Nope. Not a one."

Her face blanked out in apparent disbelief for a moment before she laughed, shaking her head at him. "Wow. You really *must* wank a lot."

Dex laughed, too. It felt good to know that he'd helped banish that stricken look from earlier, even if his brain was slowly dying from lack of adequate blood supply.

A clapping sound interrupted their laughter. "Okay, ladies and gentlemen, time to put the paintbrushes down and share your masterpieces with your group."

She quirked an eyebrow at him. "So what have you got?"

Dex glanced at the canvas filled with a giant pink mouth. The paint was still wet giving it the glossiness that had kept him awake at nights. It kinda looked like the toddler version of a Rolling Stones album cover.

"It's no Michelangelo," he murmured as he spun it around for Harper to see.

Her eyes darted over his offering. "It's a little pop-artish," she mused, "but not bad for someone who can't draw a stick figure."

Her compliment went straight to his dick. "I had the right inspiration." Her mouth—*her addictive mouth*—curved upward into a sexy smile, and that went straight to his dick, too.

"Flattery will get you nowhere."

Dex grinned. He wasn't so sure about that. She looked pretty damned chuffed with his subject matter. "Your turn. I showed you mine. Time to show me yours."

She blinked at her canvas as if she was seeing it for the first time. "I'm not sure what it is," she said after long moments. "It started out as a rainforest but…" She trailed off as she turned the painting around.

Dex took in the visual feast. Rich green leaves of varying

size and hue framed the painting. Water droplets sparkled and glistened off some of the leaves, tiny faces and eyes peered out from the foliage. The greenery encroached on the centrepiece that looked very much like the *H* of a goalpost.

But there was nothing *rugby* about it.

It looked more maypole than goalpost, with vines of green and gold twisting around the uprights and bright tropical flowers blooming intermittently. A dozen tiny ring-tailed possums hung off the crossbar in varying poses, all clearly enjoying themselves.

It was stunningly detailed. Dex's gaze scanned the canvas relentlessly, left to right, up and down. Each time, a pair of eyes he hadn't seen before became obvious, or the bright splash of a flower revealed itself. It was utterly enthralling.

Most definitely *lush*. The kind of place where he could picture Adam and Eve. Or Tarzan and Jane. Steamy. Primal.

"Is that a goalpost?" he asked when he eventually dragged his eyes off her canvas.

"Yeah. Not sure where that came from."

Dex chuckled at her obvious confusion. "I think Freud might have a field day with that."

"You think it's phallic?" She inspected the painting again before shaking her head at him. "Of course, you're a man. You think everything's phallic."

Dex smiled, unabashed. "Can I keep it?"

"Oh." Her mouth formed a surprised, lush *O*, drawing Dex's gaze. "Sure, if you want."

"This is the part where you exclaim that you simply must have my work of art, too," he teased.

Harper laughed. "But of course."

"Here, I'll even sign it," he said, dipping a fine paintbrush in the pot of black. "You sign yours, too."

He quickly scrawled *Dex the Stud* in the bottom right hand corner before presenting it to her. She'd just gone with plain *Harper* but she'd painted a little heart where the *A* should have been.

"Oh boy." She pressed her hand to her breast in faux excitement. "Now I have a signed Dexter Blake original. It'll be worth a fortune in a few years."

"Yeah," Dex snorted. "I'm sure someone will buy it for ten bucks on eBay. Maybe a hundred if we win the premiership."

"Sell it? *Never,*" she decried, keeping up her act. "I definitely need a mouth like that in my life."

Dex's gaze once again zeroed in on her mouth. "Don't we all."

Their eyes locked for a beat or two, and he swore he could hear her breath thicken before the chiming of her phone interrupted them. Harper tensed as she glanced at it like it was a boa constrictor slithering out of her canvas. "Is that her?" Dex asked.

"Yes."

"Don't look at it."

"I'm not," she said, picking up her wineglass and taking a mouthful.

He held out his hand. "Give it to me. I'll delete it."

She shook her head as she placed her glass on the table and picked up her phone. "No need." She tapped her screen a few times then put her phone down. "Gone."

Gone, yes. But not forgotten. The lightness of the mood had evaporated. It was hard to believe that they'd been talking about spank banks mere minutes ago.

The coals of anger stirred in Dex's chest. Harper was gorgeous. She may not fit the screwed-up societal notion of what constituted beauty these days, but to him, she was a fucking *goddess*. Hell, if he thought he could sleep with her and not want more, he'd be dragging her out of the restaurant right now. *By her hair, if necessary*.

A primal surge of possessiveness grabbed him by the

balls.

"You shouldn't have to put up with that crap," he growled.

"It's fine. I'm used to it."

She was putting on a brave face, but the texts had obviously gotten to her. She shouldn't have to be *used to it*. On impulse he said, "Let's do this again."

Damned if he was going to sit here and watch her crumple when she should be sitting tall, working her assets like a fucking boss.

"Paint?"

He shook his head. "Date."

"Dex." Her voice was low and husky, her imminent rejection obvious. "That's very sweet of you but I'm a big girl—clearly." She laughed, but there was a brittle edge to it. "I don't need any more pity dates. I'm fine." She reached out and squeezed his hand. "*Really*."

The conviction in her voice was solid, and he believed her. She certainly didn't seem like she was about to fall apart.

But, *screw that*, he was committed now.

It wasn't as if dating her—even for show—would be any kind of hardship.

"Don't you want to get up their noses? Chuck and your stepmother. Just a little bit?"

She smiled and her entire face lit up. "Only for the last thirteen years."

Dex lit up on the inside. He shouldn't be doing this. She was the very definition of playing with fire. But Chuck Nugent and the horse he rode in on could go and screw himself. "So let's do this. Let's date. Let's give them something to really get their panties in a wad about."

"I thought you didn't date?"

"I don't."

"But you're prepared to"—she smiled—"make the sacrifice for me?"

Dex dropped his gaze to her boobs, lingering deliberately before lifting again. "It's a tough job."

Her smile slipped as she eyed him dubiously. "What does dating entail, exactly?"

"We meet socially on a few occasions. Hang out. Have some fun while pissing off Chuck."

She regarded him for long moments. "That it?"

"You want more?" Dex tried desperately *not* to think about more. About how addictive *more* could be with Harper Nugent.

"It's *your* plan." She shrugged. "I just think we need to set the parameters before we decide to go for it. Or not."

As far as Dex was concerned, he wanted everything. All of her. Spread out on his bed. Plastered against the tiles in his shower. Bent over his dining room table. He wanted her hot and wet and needy. He wanted his name on her lips and the smell of their sex on her skin.

And if this were five years from now, then it'd be perfect. *But it wasn't.*

She was right. He needed to keep his head. If they did this, they needed to establish some ground rules. For himself more than anyone else.

"I think we should keep it platonic."

Said no sane man in the presence of a goddess ever. Except him, apparently. Jesus, Linc would kick his ass if he could hear Dex now.

"Okay." She nodded. "So it's just an evil plan to make Chuck and Anthea spit nails for a little bit?"

"Yep." Dex grinned. "You got it one."

"No fucking?"

The question stroked along his dick with all the potency of a physical caress. Why was hearing a dirty word from a pretty mouth such a frickin' turn-on?

Dex swallowed as he shook his head. "*Definitely* no

fucking. Not that I don't want to," he hastened to assure her, in case the words of her evil stepmother were still holding some kind of sway. "Trust me, there's nothing I want more right now then to strip you out of your clothes, lay you on this table, upend that glass of wine over you and lick it out of every nook and cranny, and to hell with everyone here watching."

It was gratifying to see her swallow. To see the slight widening of her eyes and the brisk dilation of her pupils. To hear the husky tremble in her voice as she said, "Okay."

"I just can't afford the distraction of sex with you, Harper, because…man…" He stared at her mouth. "I have a very bad feeling that I might not want to stop. But…hanging out? That I can do."

Of course he could. He may still want to relieve her of her clothes, but that didn't mean he couldn't control himself. Especially when he'd gone to all the trouble of setting the ground rules.

She nodded. "Okay."

Her voice was still husky, and Dex wanted to beat his chest like fucking Tarzan because he'd managed to turn Harper on just by describing how he wanted to do her on the table in front of everyone.

"Whaddya reckon?" He grinned, raising his almost empty beer bottle. "Want to screw with Chuckie?"

She lifted her almost empty wineglass and tapped it against the bottle. "Fucking A."

Dex grinned. Now all he had to do was keep his hands—and his tongue—to himself.

Chapter Four

I have a very bad feeling I might not want to stop.

Harper was still thinking about those words two days later as she painted the scales on a mermaid's tail. The under-the-sea mural dominated the expanse of wall just inside the doors of the ward. Public bathrooms interrupted the flow of the wall, but Harper had framed the doorways with sparkly seaweed, curious starfish and luminescent seashells, making them part of the watery landscape.

The mural was her best yet. Even if she did say so herself.

Octopus's Garden and *Rock Lobster* were playing on repeat via her ear buds because there was nothing like mood music when she was painting. It also blocked out the eerie silence of the empty ward, devoid of patients and the hustle bustle of hospital life while she completed the mural. This area would be done early next week, and the ward was scheduled to reopen by week's end.

So she was alone. With her thoughts. Her very *indecent* thoughts. Unfortunately, no amount of Beatles or eighties pop could drown out her memories, or the conversation that had played on a loop in her head since Wednesday night.

I have a very bad feeling I might not want to stop.

Christ, the man had almost made her come from that phrase alone. He certainly had when she'd gotten home from the restaurant and she'd collapsed on her bed, reaching into her bedside drawer for some relief from the tingling pressure between her legs. She'd shut her eyes and imagined him saying it over and over as she'd touched herself.

Imagined *him* lying on *his* bed, touching *himself* with those long, slow strokes.

Just as well they were being platonic because if he ever actually touched her with any sexual intent, she'd probably go off like a bloody firework. Just thinking about him now had her body tingling deliciously.

But no. Their dates were fake. For show only.

Absolutely, under no circumstances, did they involve fucking.

God. Harper still couldn't believe she'd agreed to date Dexter Blake. Even fake dating as they were, it was hard to get her head around it. She just hoped she could *keep* her head and remember that there was a purpose to their strange little arrangement—messing with Chuck and her stepmum.

Harper smiled just thinking about it. Every time she thought they were crazy, she thought of Chuck's face when he found out his stepsister was dating one of the stars of the Sydney Smoke rugby team, and a shot of pure evil glee lit up her system like the splashes of glitter paint she'd added to the mural to make the yellow sand of the ocean floor sparkle.

It was hard to believe now how desperate she'd been to like Chuck in the beginning. To have him like her. And she'd been so sure that he did. But then she'd overheard him telling his friend that Harper would squash him if she sat on him.

It had hurt. And crushed all her hopes for having a big brother to look out for her.

A tap on Harper's shoulder coincided with a flicker in her peripheral vision, scaring her witless. She leaped back, ripping her ear buds out. It was a couple of seconds before the mist of fright cleared enough that she realised who it was.

"Hey."

"Shit, Dex," she gasped, clutching her chest, her heart thumping like a bongo drum. "You scared the bejesus out of me."

"Sorry." He held his hands up in surrender, but the laughter in his gaze belied the apology.

"What the hell are you doing here?"

Had her horny vibes conjured him up? God knew they were pretty damn powerful, if the constant electric hum of her body was anything to go by. She wanted to touch him to see if he was real, but damn if the man didn't look good enough to eat. She wasn't going to risk touching him in case she grabbed him and took a bloody great bite.

He was in casual shorts and his silver and blue Smoke jersey, tight in the shoulders and snug against his chest. It was clean and smelled of sunshine and laundry detergent, unlike the night he'd *rescued* her from Chuck, when it had been covered in grass and dirt and smelled like sweat and muscle liniment.

Smokin' hot—the team's catchphrase—didn't even begin to describe him.

She, on the other hand, looked a wreck. She was wearing her baggy overalls, which zipped up at the front and left *everything* to the imagination. Her hair was scraped back into a high, messy ponytail, and there was, no doubt, paint in it somewhere.

There was *always* paint in her hair.

"Just finishing up a scheduled visit to some of the wards. The different teams in the comp do it regularly."

"That's very cool," she said.

"Yeah. It's good fun. Except for the media that follow us around asking dumb questions and taking a zillion pictures, which makes it feel fake. I was kind of over them, so I thought I'd slip away and see if I could find you."

"Oh." Harper didn't know what to say. They'd agreed to do something on Sunday afternoon. The Smoke played on Saturday night, and he was going to text her the next day with some plans. She hadn't figured she'd see him until then.

Except in her dirty, dirty mind.

The fact that he was here, seeking her out, was... interesting. Also, just a little bit thrilling.

"Man..." His gaze wandered over her from head to toe. "You look *good*."

Harper glanced down at herself. "I...do?"

He nodded as his gaze zeroed in on the front zipper. "You do."

"I'm in tatty, baggy old overalls and have paint on my hands and in my hair. I smell like I've taken a bath in turpentine."

"Yeah," he murmured, his gaze slowly returning to her face. "Who knew that was such a sexy combination?"

His lopsided smile caused her heart to skip a beat. Heat crept up her chest and neck, and she was thankful for the thick material of her overalls as her nipples tightened in blatant response.

He dragged in a breath and shoved his hands in his pockets. "Well, come on, woman, tell me about the damn mural before I do something impulsive."

Impulsive? Like what?

The low growl twirled and twined itself around internal muscles with a gossamer touch, sparking to life all the pent-up lust she'd been trying to control the last couple of days.

Harper wiped the scenarios from her mind's eye with a quick clearing of her throat. "This is my...under-the-sea mural," she said, jerking into action. She wandered down to where it started, sucking in some much needed air as she fought to control her reaction to his nearness.

It was insanity of the highest order how easily Dexter Blake could affect her body. No man had ever left her panting with his presence alone.

Determined to keep this aboveboard and professional in her *workplace,* she explained succinctly and methodically what she was trying to achieve. She pretended he was one of her school-age art students and not a fully-grown man who was emitting so much testosterone she was almost faint with it.

She discussed colour and technique and where she was going with the bare sketches on the unfinished section as her pulse fluttered madly. Some would have called it babbling. But she had to engage her mouth in something useful lest it develop a mind of its own.

She was too aware of him to relax. Too aware of his hands jammed in his pockets, his gaze on her mouth as she talked… his heated interest in her zipper.

His cursory questions and complete disinterest in the answers seemed merely an excuse to let his gaze wander freely over her. He didn't touch her, but she felt the hot, sticky fingerprints of his attention mark every part of her body.

Christ. He was turning her on just by *looking* at her.

"Okay," she said, her voice tremulous with desire as she ran out of scintillating factoids about the mural. He needed to stop or *she* was going to do something impulsive. "I think it's time you left now."

To his credit he didn't protest, or pretend he didn't know why she was kicking him out. He nodded. "I really did come down here just to say hi but… *Jesus.*" His gaze dropped again to her zipper. "Are you wearing anything under that?"

A twinge, like the low, sexy notes of a saxophone,

undulated across her pelvic floor. Dex was looking at her like he wanted to peel her out of her overalls as if she were a ripe banana. God knew he could do it easily. He was only an arm's length away. He could just reached out and yank if he wanted.

Harper swallowed. Her breath hitched. "Well, I'm not naked, if that's what you mean."

His low groan rubbed against her skin like the finest grade sandpaper, her nipples beading painfully against the fabric of her bra. "Damn."

The word rumbled out of him, arrowing heat from her breasts directly to the bullseye between her legs. She should send him on his way for both their sanities — push him out the door and tell him she'd see him on Sunday — but the desire darkening his usually light green eyes was a heady thing.

"I'm wearing underwear," she clarified quickly, as if it might give some protection from the incendiary gaze threatening to melt her overalls right off.

"Christ," he muttered, his gaze once more zeroing in on the tab of her zipper as he reefed a hand out of his pocket and jammed it through his hair. "All I can think about is yanking that damn zip down."

It was all she could think about, too.

Harper's breath was thick as fog in her throat, her pulse slowing. He took a step toward her.

"Tell me to go," he murmured, his gaze, almost feral now, on her mouth.

Harper couldn't. She was virtually paralysed with lust. How she was managing to stay upright under his thorough eye-fucking she had no idea.

"No."

She should. But she couldn't.

It was like an invisible string pulled them inexorably together, and she didn't have the power or the will to break it. He was going to have to man up if he wanted out of here unmolested.

"*Jesus, Harper,*" he whispered, looking at her for long moments, looking into her eyes this time as if he was searching for some kind of lifeline.

She clocked the exact second he stopped searching.

"Goddamn it," he swore, taking the one pace necessary to cover the distance between them, his hands grasping her upper arms, yanking her toward him as his mouth closed on hers.

After days and days of sexual fantasies, the touch of his mouth was like petrol on a fire, and she blazed with need. Harper had heard other women talking about hearing the Hallelujah Chorus when the right guy kissed you. Choirs of angels and all that jazz. But that wasn't what she was hearing. There was music all right, but it was no glorious benediction. It was rock-and-freaking-roll.

It was the bourbon-gravelly tones of Nickleback singing about pants around her feet and dirt on her knees.

She was vaguely aware of him walking her backward toward the wall, her legs moving automatically at the insistent push of his powerful thighs, and she had just enough sense in her rapidly devolving thought processes to protest.

"No, no," she muttered, tearing her mouth from his. "The paint's wet."

The harsh suck of his breath was loud in her ears for the moment or two his glazed eyes raked her face before he growled in frustration and grabbed her hand, pulling her into the nearest bathroom. Harper was only vaguely aware of their surroundings, of being spun and planted firmly against a strip of wall between the doorway and a washbasin, of the disinfectant foam pump not far from her head, of the two open toilet doors over Dex's shoulder.

She was much more aware of the heaving of his chest, the rich glitter in his eyes as his gaze raked down her body, and the exciting perfume of hot, hard man. The familiar chemical smells of paint and turps were drowned out by the enthralling waft of more natural chemicals.

"I haven't been able to get you out of my head," he murmured, his gaze fixing on her zipper again.

Harper's head spun at the admission. It was an intoxicating statement, and she bunched the hand she didn't know was resting on his bicep into the fabric of his jersey. Her breath rasped as his hand stroked down the open collar of her overalls into her cleavage to toy with the tab of the zip. His fingertips brushed against the rise of her breasts as he played with it. Her nipples tightened into painfully hard points in response.

"You're driving me crazy," he said. "This *tab* is driving me crazy."

Harper knew exactly how he felt. Thoughts of Dex had occupied a stupid amount of her time. Thoughts of him soothing the painful ache of her nipples with his tongue were *all* she could think about now.

The give of the first tooth was louder than the husky saw of their breathing and the jitterbug of her pulse through her ears. Harper's gaze fell on the cheekbones of his bowed head as he tugged some more, tracking the progress, watching his handiwork—watching the zipper cede to his insistent downward tug, and the slow reveal of her underwear.

Somewhere in the sludge that was now her brain, she was thankful she'd chosen to wear a matching set today.

Her overalls slowly parted to reveal all of her, and Harper moaned as he anchored the zipper at its southernmost point, his fingers brushing softly against her crotch.

"Oh yes," Dex whispered, his voice reverential, his head still bowed. "God *yes.*"

He slid his hands inside her overalls. Her breath hitched. Nerve endings beneath her skin twitched at his touch. "I knew you'd look like this," he said, his hands sliding north, gliding over the cups of her bra and squeezing.

She gasped this time, her back arching involuntarily, her shoulder blades still anchored to the wall as her hips, the same height as his, ground against him. He ground back, the hard ridge of his cock hitting her in just the right spot.

"*Fuck*," he groaned, burying his face in her neck.

"*Mmhgnh*," she muttered unintelligibly, grinding again, finding some relief for the pressure building to fever pitch between her legs.

Her eyes practically rolled back in her head as he yanked her bra cups aside, his greedy hands each claiming a breast. They ground on each other like horny teenagers, and Harper moaned as he dropped soft kisses down her neck, into the hollow of her throat. She whimpered as he traced a wet path lower. When his mouth found a nipple, she cried out, a violent clenching between her legs bringing her out of her sexual stupor.

If they didn't stop this now, she was going to come embarrassingly quickly. Possibly even right now. Not to mention the fact she never let men she barely knew unzip her and suck on her nipples.

Hell, they weren't supposed to even be *doing* this.

"This isn't starting very well at all," she panted, concentrating hard on sounding reasonable as he sucked, so damn good, on her nipple. "We seem to be well and truly breaking the ground rules."

Which was putting it mildly. The ground rules were lying in smoking rubble at their feet.

He released his mouthful, panting as he straightened to look her in the eye for long moments, potent male frustration brimming in his gaze. "Maybe we can bend them a little?"

Harper struggled to sound normal instead of someone who'd just had her nipple sucked by a goddamn *Jedi*. "*Bend* them?"

He nodded. "I know you're not averse to a spot of masturbation. Why not let me help you with that?"

The hands on her breasts moved south, the fingers trekking over her belly to dip just under the lacy edge of underwear.

So much for not letting him near her lady parts. If they could talk, they'd be begging him to come closer.

Her usual awkwardness over the softness of her belly and the roundness of her hips was nowhere to be seen. All that existed was sensation. It felt so damn good, Harper had to squeeze her legs together to stop from coming there and then.

He wanted to get her off? *Hell-fucking-yeah.* She was too far-gone to deny him *or* herself. She'd think about the reasons and the implications later.

After.

"As long as it's mutual," she said, grabbing for the hard length of his cock, jammed between them and still taunting her in all the right places.

The way his eyes shut tight, and the guttural desperation of his strangled groan went straight to the part of her that was 100 percent female, and she squeezed him through his shorts.

"*Christ,*" he swore under his breath, his eyes pinging open. "Abso-frickin-lutely."

His hand pushed past that lacy border and slid, in one easy movement, into the slick heat between her legs. The sensation tore through her like an electric current, and she cried out as she bucked against the blissful invasion of his fingers.

"God," he groaned, his lips at her neck again, his warm breath spreading goose bumps down her throat and prickling in her scalp as his finger swirled languorously. "You're *so* wet."

Harper had been wet all damn week.

And his light, gentle touch wasn't nearly enough for what she needed. She squirmed against his hand, grinding, wanting more. "You want it harder, huh?" he murmured, and she gasped as his fingers suddenly became serious, dropping all the pansy-assed swirling and ploughing hard and true, straight to the erect knot of nerves he was seeking.

She gasped and bucked when he found it, shoving a hand into the hair at his nape and crying out when he rubbed— hanging on tight to him as he rubbed and rubbed, relentless in his quest.

"Yes," she moaned over and over, squeezing his cock in her hand reflexively. His corresponding groan filled up her senses and expanded in her chest, and she delved frantically inside his shorts, needing suddenly, *desperately*, to feel him, to touch him, to wrap her hand around all that velvet steeliness.

"*Fuuuck*," he groaned as she hit pay dirt and quickly— greedily—slid her hand up and down the length of him.

Then his mouth was on hers and they were kissing hard and deep and wet, and they were moaning and rubbing and tugging and grinding. Harper's heart crashed in her chest and her pulse roared in her ears and her breathing came in shallow gasps and her breasts were squashed against his chest and they were in a goddamn bathroom at her *work* and she didn't care.

Only his hot, frantic kisses and the build of tension inside her pelvis mattered in a world that had narrowed down to just the two of them. The rub of his finger on her clit, the slide of her hand on his cock, the frantic noises they were making at the backs of their throats as they kissed on a far deeper level than just their mouths.

Deeper than Harper had ever been kissed before.

Somewhere inside her, lost to the insanity that was lust, she knew it was significant. That everything about this man was significant. But that part did not have the con right now. Her clitoris was driving the bus, and it demanded all her attention as it hurtled her recklessly toward the station.

Which didn't take much longer. The moment he slid two fingers inside her, all the pressure that had been building and coiling tight in her thighs and belly released in a sudden pop, and Harper was flung into the heavens.

She wrenched her mouth away, throwing her head back against the wall as she flew. Dex rubbed harder, quicker, and she reciprocated, increasing the slide of her hand on his cock, knowing from the tremble of his biceps and quads and the deep guttural edge to his groans that he was close.

Suddenly his hips jerked to a halt. A loud bellow ripped from his throat. Harper milked him harder, faster, crying out in pleasure *and* triumph as he came, too, spurting hot in her hand.

Her eyes were shut, but with her hand still firmly anchored at Dex's nape they spiralled together, the pleasure so intense it felt like it was never going to end. She wanted to slow it right down, coast along with him through the wonder of it and marvel at the magic they'd created.

It felt like they'd been plunged into a rainbow, or maybe even seen the face of God. Harper wasn't a religious person, but if anything was going to convert her, coming apart with Dex like this would do it.

They seemed to drift through the thrall forever, and it wasn't until the chime of an incoming text message interrupted the moment that Harper came back to herself. Dex had collapsed against her, his full weight pinning her to the wall, his ragged breath hot at her neck. His hand was still in her pants, his semi-erect cock still in her hand, and his come was splattered over both of them.

She was a hot, sticky mess, and she'd never felt so damn *good*. So damn desired.

Powerful and female and wanton.

Harper could only begin to imagine how good she'd feel if their bits ever got to bump together for real. He had a lot going on between his legs, and while his fingers had sufficed this time, she sure as hell wanted *that* all up in her business.

"It isn't mine," she said eventually, when the chime sounded again.

"It's mine," he said, his lips brushing her neck, his voice muffled. "It'll be one of the guys."

He roused himself, his hand sliding out of her underwear to her hip, gripping it as he rocked his weight back on the balls of his feet, the handful of him she had sliding from her grasp.

"Well…" he said, looking down at himself, his voice still husky, "that was…"

"Messy?"

He huffed out a laugh, but Harper was secretly delighted to see he looked as mystified by what had just happened as she was. "Yeah."

"Intense," she offered.

He shoved a hand through his hair, his gaze locking with hers. "Definitely."

A beat or two passed before his phone chimed again. He rolled his eyes, tucking himself back into his shorts as he reached behind for his mobile.

"Apparently we're making an extra stop-off at the hospital radio station," he said, reading the text. "And my absence has been noted."

Harper's head was still spinning, her legs still unsteady as she acknowledged his summons. "You'd better go then."

He grimaced as he glanced at her, but it died as his gaze lit on her still gaping overalls and her bared breasts, the pulled-aside cups giving them the kind of support usually only found at the end of a surgeon's knife.

"Yeah…but I don't want to," Dex muttered.

She was grateful for the support of the wall behind her as his heated gaze turned her legs back to jelly. He was staring at her like he wanted seconds.

Possibly with some chocolate topping.

He took a step toward her, but Harper threw her hand—the clean one—up to halt the movement. It landed on his chest, the muscle big and meaty beneath her palm. It took all her willpower not to curl her fingers into it.

"No," she said, her voice still raspy. "Duty calls."

For *both* of them. She was at work for fuck's sake. It wasn't uncommon for people to drop in to check on her progress, or even just to chat.

His frustrated gaze roamed over her face then back to her breasts again. It might as well have been his tongue for the way her nipples preened and burgeoned beneath his scrutiny. She felt the subtle tensing of his pec and locked her wrist, ready to repel him should he pounce.

Although, God knew, her nipples would probably win the argument between duty and lust if he really decided to push the boundary.

His phone chimed again and he growled—actually *growled*—low in the back of his throat. "Fine," he huffed, the taut muscle relaxing beneath her palm before he reached over, yanked her zip up and took a step back.

He looked down at himself again. His jersey had escaped most of the load he'd shot only a minute ago, but some repair was clearly needed. He took a step toward the basin and looked at himself in the half mirror.

"How am I going to explain that?"

"Maybe not the truth," Harper smiled.

He laughed. "Are you kidding? I just came in about ten seconds flat. I don't think I'll be bragging about that one."

"Best damn ten seconds of my life," she said. He glanced sidelong at her in the mirror and smiled. "Here." She pulled a wad of paper towels out of the dispenser, flicking on the tap to wet them slightly before handing them over. He dabbed at the stains as she washed her hands and tended to her own mess, not that they could be really detected amidst all the caked on paint.

"I think I just made it worse," Dex grimaced, inspecting the results in the mirror.

"Sorry," Harper said, chewing on the inside of her cheek to keep from laughing. "Next time, I'll get down on my knees."

He glanced up sharply with a swift intake of breath. His gaze dropped to her mouth with such intensity she was left in no doubt he was thinking about her lips moving up and down his dick. "Christ," he said, shaking his head at the grin she couldn't suppress. "Are you *trying* to make me come again?"

Harper laughed this time. "Sorry. Just a little something for your spank bank."

"Already there," he said, the admission causing a tight, hot tingle low in her belly. He dragged his attention from her mouth back to the mirror, making a dissatisfied noise at the back of his throat.

"Here, try this," Harper said, filling her cupped hand with the running tap water and splashing it at the affected area.

He jumped back as the water soaked in, gaping at her then at his jersey then back at her. "How does that make it better?"

"Just say you were washing your hands like a good boy and the tap sprayed up at you. They're pretty notorious for that."

He shook his head as he looked in the mirror again. "They're never going to believe me."

"Fine," she murmured, amused at his despair as she pulled off more paper towels for him to clean up the excess water. "Tell them Chuck Nugent's stepsister jerked you off in a bathroom while they were visiting sick and injured kiddies and playing nice for the cameras."

He grabbed the hand towel and mopped at the wet patch. "I don't kiss and tell," he growled.

"Oh, I see," she teased. "You just want to keep me as your dirty little secret."

Dex threw the paper towel in the bin before flicking the tap off with a quick swat. He grabbed her by the baggy front of her overalls and hauled her close. "Fucking A," he growled, his mouth landing on hers in a brief, punishing kiss.

Harper was useless against the onslaught, grasping his biceps and moaning her capitulation, almost falling backward when he released her just as abruptly. "Will you be watching the game tomorrow?"

She nodded. It was about all she was capable of currently. "Yes."

His gaze locked with hers. "What will you be wearing?"

Harper's breath hitched, and she was unable to look away from the fever she saw in his eyes. "What do you want me to wear?"

He glanced down at the zipper. "Nothing."

Her belly tightened. "Okay."

"I want you stretched out on your couch, naked in front of the television."

"Okay."

"I want you to slide your dildo in and keep it there for the entire game, and every time we score a try I want you to come."

Harper was pretty damn sure she was about to come right now. She'd never been given homework by a guy before—erotic or otherwise—and she was so turned on she could barely see straight. She supposed she should be shocked. She'd known him for such a short time, and they were in a supposedly fake *platonic* relationship.

She *should* tell him to go to hell. But *screw that.*

"Okay."

"I want to know that while I'm *sweating* my ass off on that field that you're at home *getting* your ass off. Will you do that for me, Harper?"

She swallowed. "Okay."

Long moments passed as they stared at each other. Her heart tripped manically in her chest and at all her pulse points. Her breath came in rough pants. Harper wondered if the heat and hunger she could see in Dex's eyes was his, or merely a reflection of her own arousal.

He nodded, satisfied. "Good. See you Sunday."

Then he stepped around her and walked out the door, leaving Harper entirely unfit to paint anything.

Chapter Five

Harper was killing anything that crossed her path.

Nothing better for an attack of the nerves than jumping on the PlayStation and kicking some Battlefront ass while she waited for Dex to pick her up.

She'd been a gamer since her teens—much to Anthea's displeasure—and if it wasn't for the twins and Em making demands on her time, she'd probably be one of those sad basement-dwellers wearing stained trackies, surrounded by take-away cartons and floor to ceiling bottled water in case the zombie apocalypse actually happened while she was questing with online friends in World of Warcraft.

Right now, it felt good to be blowing shit up. Gave her something else to think about.

The Sydney Smoke had lost their game last night but had still managed to score four tries. Which meant she was going to have to look Dex in the eye when he got here, knowing *he knew* exactly what she'd been doing during those eighty minutes.

On Friday, and even last night in the midst of it all, it had been thrilling to perform such an illicit act in the privacy of her own apartment. Naughty. And...liberating. But having to face Dex knowing that *he knew* what she'd done? That was an entirely different matter.

There was a rap on the door. Her suddenly nerveless fingers paused the game before the controller clattered onto the coffee table.

Dex. Five o'clock. On the dot. Heat flooded Harper's face. *God.* What was she doing with him? What was he doing with her?

A second knock yanked her out of her inertia. She rose off the couch automatically, her legs moving mechanically to the door. Thoughts twirled round and round in her brain like a spinning top.

Be cool. You're an adult. You're both adults. You're single. He's single. You're allowed to play games. Sexual *games. You haven't done* anything *wrong.*

"Hey," he said, as she swung the door open, one big hand sliding up high on the doorframe, his gaze speculative as he looked her up and down in a way that left her in no doubt as to what he was thinking.

"Hey," she said back, a little breathless from the dirty in his smile.

She had the crazy urge to lean forward and kiss him on the cheek. As a...greeting. After all, she *had* gotten naked and masturbated last night—*four* times—because *he'd* asked her to. But something stopped her. Kissing him on the cheek? That seemed a little too...familiar.

She didn't know if they had *that* kind of relationship.

She settled for checking him out instead. Like her, he was in jeans and a T-shirt—perfect attire for the drive-in movie they were seeing. His shirt was light gray, his jeans a soft, distressed blue that appeared to be more from age than any kind of design intent. His smile was smooth, his stubble was rough, and he smelled like he'd been dipped in cinnamon sugar.

Her own personal churro.

Even the slight puffiness of his left eye where he'd copped an elbow last night added to his sex appeal.

He wore the hell out of all of it.

"Does it hurt?" she asked, nodding at the injury.

He shook his head as he pressed gently around the orbit. "Nah. Had worse."

She'd seen enough images of him online with blood pouring out of his head to believe him. "I'll just go grab my bag."

He nodded, and Harper was conscious he'd followed her into the apartment. Conscious of his gaze burning a hole in the rump of her jeans. She wished she'd worn the longer shirt now. Showing off the ass he'd already confessed to liking had seemed like a good idea a couple of hours ago but now that he was two paces behind her, not so much.

Harper was snatching up her bag off the lounge when he said, "Now *that's* what I call a television."

"Oh...yes." She'd bought the unit specifically with her gaming habit in mind. She also had large dual computer screens for her online gaming.

The game she'd been playing was still frozen on the screen, and she strode toward it to turn it off.

"That must be what? Seventy inches?"

"Eighty."

He stuck his hands on his hips and glanced at her. "You sure know how to intimidate a man."

Harper snorted. She knew for a fact that Dexter Blake had no reason to be intimidated.

"You game?" he asked as she picked up the controller.

"Yep."

He grinned at her. "Harper Nugent, you just get more

and more awesome."

It was hardly romantic or flowery, but Harper buzzed all over from the compliment, her rib cage suddenly too small to contain the surge of pride rising in her chest. She grinned back, recognising the zeal of a fellow gamer in Dex's eyes. "You play, too?"

"I'm a more recent convert, although it's been a while."

"Battlefront?" she asked, cocking her head toward the screen.

"Hell yeah." He glanced at his watch, the fingers of the other hand drumming against his thigh. "We still have an hour before we absolutely *have* to leave. Fancy a game?"

Considering he'd had the upper hand in the *games* they'd already played, Harper was more than keen to partake of one where she felt in control. "Sure," she said casually.

"You any good?"

Harper gave her very best nonchalant shrug as she crossed to the long, low television cabinet and dragged out another cordless controller. "I do okay."

He narrowed his eyes as she passed it to him. "You're going to kick my ass, aren't you?"

She bit the inside of her cheek to stop from laughing as she walked to the couch and sat. "I can be gentle with you if you like."

"I would like," he said, sitting down beside her. The couch was a long three-seater, deep, with generous cushions. She'd sat just off-centre of the middle, and Dex had done the same, about a foot separating them.

"Of course, you are injured after all," she murmured, leaning forward at the hips as she snatched her controller off the coffee table and navigated to a new map. "You want to play as a team, or you want me to kick your ass first?"

He laughed. "Bring it."

"All right then. Don't say I didn't warn you." Harper

grinned. "Prepare to be annihilated." Her fingers moved quickly on the controller as she set things up. She glanced across at him. "You ready?"

Dex stretched out his traps. "I was born ready, baby."

Harper pressed play, and they were off, sitting forward, shoulders hunched, brows furrowed. Dex did a cute thing where he stuck his tongue out whenever he was about to shoot. It made it easier for Harper to pre-empt, but still it took her twenty minutes to get him just where she wanted him. If this was him rusty, then he must have been damn good at one stage.

She was closing in on him, going in for the fatal blow when he said, "Is this where you did the deed last night?"

Harper startled at the unexpected question and misfired. His guy blasted a bunch of hers. She paused the game, and he grinned as she looked at him.

"Are you doing this on purpose, to try and put me off my game?"

"Damn straight," he said, completely unabashed, looking boyish suddenly. "Is it working?"

It most certainly was. Her concentration was shot now she'd been brought out of the virtual world to face the real world and the real man sitting beside her.

"It was, wasn't it?" he insisted, harking back to his original question.

It would have been handy to be able to muster a glare, but the fact that it was, in fact, the place where she had *done the deed*, put Harper on the back foot.

"I have a blush that tells me it was." He looked up and down the length of the couch then back at her, his gaze lowering to her mouth. "I'm sorry I couldn't have made it more than four for you but we were robbed with a couple of those penalties."

Harper was relieved the Smoke had only run the ball

over that many times. She wasn't sure she'd been hydrated enough for a fifth orgasm.

"So…how was it?"

There was no way she was telling him last night had been the single most risqué thing she'd ever done. Or the thrill of it alone had kept her excitement at fever pitch between tries.

He'd held the upper hand in this conversation far too long.

Recovering her composure, Harper injected some steel into her spine. She leaned in slightly and lowered her voice. "You want a…blow by blow?"

His big smile oozed sex and confidence. "Hell yeah."

"I videoed it if you want to watch?"

His sudden stillness, and the bob of his throat as he sat even more forward, were gratifying. "You…did?"

Harper dropped her head to the side and shot him a *gotcha* smile before pressing start and blasting his last man to smithereens while he was still staring at her. "Oops." She turned to him and batted her eyelids as GAME OVER flashed on the screen. "Sorry."

He laughed then. Big and deep. "You like to play dirty."

She arched an eyebrow. "I'm learning to play by your rules."

He grinned. "Oh, this is going to be so much fun."

Harper rolled her eyes at his obvious enjoyment. "Another?"

"Sure. But let's play as a team this time. At least until I'm not so rusty anymore. Then I'll kick *your* ass, paint girl."

"Ha!" Harper said, setting up another game. "Dream on, rugby."

They didn't go to the drive-in. The time came to leave and

they were in the middle of a battle against enemy insurgents, and they decided to just keep playing. Harper grabbed two beers and some corn chips and salsa, and they worked their way through dozens of levels together.

Dinnertime came and they ordered pizza. They devoured two between them and drank more beer. Harper couldn't remember the last time she'd had this much fun.

With her clothes on anyway.

It was ten before they were triumphant in their third map together.

"Another?" Harper asked.

He was lounging back on the couch, his legs wide apart in that potently casual way of men. His T-shirt fell flat against the planes of his belly, and his jeans clung like a second skin, stretched out over thick quads and cupping the bulge of what she knew to be a decent size package at the juncture of his thighs. Every line and angle of his body reflected a man relaxed and content, like a big jungle cat, stretched out all loose-limbed, his stomach full.

Except his eyes. There was nothing content about those. They were much more alert. Much more...carnal. Up until now, the only thing that had charged the atmosphere had been a keen sense of competition. But it had been companionable.

Matey. Blokey, even.

But those eyes made her wary. And just a little bit horny.

"Sure," he said, still casual. "Want to make it interesting?"

"Ah, you want to battle *me*, huh? Feeling confident again?"

He grinned. "I think I have my mojo back."

As if he'd ever lost it. "All right then," she said, leaning forward, elbows on her knees as she set up a battle between the two of them.

"Can I suggest a variation?"

Harper looked over her shoulder at him. "A variation?"

He nodded, his eyes glittering now. "Strip Battlefront is kinda fun."

Her breath stuttered to a halt somewhere between her lungs and her mouth. "Strip Battlefront?"

"Sure." He grinned. "The guys and I play it *all* the time."

She relaxed slightly at his teasing tone. The thought of a bunch of buck naked rugby players striping off their clothes in front of a video game was amusing as hell. "Oh really? That's funny," she mused. "None of *my* guy friends have ever suggested it."

"I'm sure they wanted to."

Harper snorted. "I doubt it." She often got together with a bunch of other gamer friends and pulled all-nighters.

"Are they gay?"

"Only a couple of them."

His gaze dropped briefly to where the V of her T-shirt skimmed her cleavage before returning to her face. "So, just stupid then?"

Harper smiled at the compliment. Dexter Blake was good for her ego. "I prefer gentlemen."

It was his turn to snort, and Harper wasn't left in any doubt that Dex thought her friends were fools. "What about your girlfriends?" he pressed. "You must have played something like that at girlie sleepovers?"

"Sure." She smiled sweetly. "Just before our naked pillow fights." Harper rolled her eyes. "In your dreams, rugby."

"You have no idea." Dex grinned. "So…what do you say? You up for it?"

Harper wished she could say she wasn't. Wished that she could say he'd shocked her and slap him across the face for suggesting something so outrageously risqué. But given what she'd done on this very couch twenty-four hours ago, it was probably a bit late to play the puritan.

And, God help her, there was something so illicitly wicked

about the thought.

Was she up for it?

Anticipation fluttered fingers over muscle fibres deep in her pelvis as her pulse tap-danced at her wrists and temple. It seemed, as far as Dex was concerned, she was up for anything. Maybe it was because she knew they weren't in any kind of a relationship that she felt like she didn't have to follow any of the relationship rules.

"You're very daring aren't you?"

He shook his head. "Only on the rugby field. And around you, it seems."

Harper tried not to let that go to her head. She failed. "How do you play it?"

His slow smile spread heat through her belly and thighs. "Simple. Every time you lose a man, you lose a piece of clothing."

Harper did a mental inventory of what they were wearing. She had a grand total of four items of clothing—they'd both discarded their shoes a long time ago. Unless Dex had a fetish for women's underwear, he only had three. Two if he was commando.

Lordy. Her heart palpitated wildly at the thought.

Given how quickly men died in the virtual world they could both be naked pretty damn quick. She'd have to be careful. None of her players could be expendable. She'd have to play it really safe.

Which was ironic given how she was doing the exact opposite in the *real* world.

Where the hell this would end up, Harper had no idea. More mutual masturbation? Or further? Wherever it was, she was pretty sure they'd just coasted on past Platonic-land.

"How do you win?"

"How do you not?" he joked, but he sobered as she shot him her best *be serious* face. "First one to naked is the loser."

Harper calculated that since she had one more piece of clothing than him, he'd probably be the first one naked. He was good, but she was better. It was a risk she was prepared to take to see him in his birthday suit.

Sure, she'd held his cock in her hand, but she'd seen precious little of him, considering. He'd seen a hell of a lot more of her through the open zip of her overalls.

"Turn the lights out while I set it up."

If she had to lose her clothes in front of him, she wasn't going to do it the bright splash of the overhead light.

"How will I see you?"

"You'll see enough," Harper said, setting her chin.

She may be doing something crazy and spontaneous, but years of self-consciousness about her body were hard to overcome, no matter how much Dex seemed into her.

And there was nothing as flattering as low light.

• • •

Dex groaned when Harper drew first blood in the second minute. She whooped and grinned at him. "Take it off, rugby."

He laughed as he hauled his shirt over his head. It was hard not to, seeing her utter glee, but he needed to pay more attention to his big head instead of the expectant buzz coursing through his little one if he wanted to keep his wits about him and his clothes on for longer than five minutes.

He'd been disappointed when she'd wanted the lights out, but the glow from the television screen was enough. In fact, the low light was kind of romantic, playing as it was in her hair, and shadowing the V of her chest not covered by T-shirt. It fell against the jut of her breasts, the line of her arms, and the dark denim of her thighs.

If she hadn't eaten off her very distracting lip gloss a couple of hours ago, it would probably be reflected in that, too.

This night was about to become a whole lot more interesting, and he, for one, couldn't wait. Ever since their rub and tug sessions the other day, he'd been dying to get her naked.

And horizontal.

God, he doubted he'd ever played as hard as he had last night on that field. The thought of Harper naked on her couch watching him, touching herself, had put a rocket on his feet and a motor in his mouth. He wasn't usually very vocal during a game. He had a job to do, and he just put his head down and did it, leaving the directions and rallying up to others.

But last night he'd been animated, desperate not just to win but to score as many tries as they could. Desperate to score one himself so the camera would zoom in on him and he could stare straight into it, and through it at Harper.

It had been a tough game and a loss was always hard, but at least this one came easier knowing that while *he* may not have scored, *Harper* sure as hell had.

"We going again?" he asked as she sat there, the game waiting patiently for her to restart it as her gaze roamed his chest. He resisted the urge to puff out like a peacock under her scrutiny.

It may have been dark, but he could see the flare of heat in the golden brown depths of her eyes, could hear the slight roughening of her breath as it fell from slightly parted lips.

Her stare slammed into his groin and jolted through his dick like an electric shock. He was stiff as a pike in seconds.

"Hmm?" She glanced at him with what appeared to be difficulty. "Oh…sure…yeah."

Dex suppressed a smile as the game restarted. He hoped she was distracted enough to make a mistake with the game, because he meant to have her clothes off as quickly as goddamn possible.

Within a minute he'd taken down one of her guys. "Your turn." He smiled, his heart thudding against his ribs, his mouth salivating at the thought of seeing her breasts again.

She hesitated for a moment before standing and peeling herself out of her jeans. It hadn't been the move he'd thought she was going to make, but he wasn't complaining as the lines of quad and calf were revealed for his viewing pleasure. She had the legs of an Amazon—long but sturdy, the muscles solid, the thighs kissingly enticing. Legs that would grip a man's waist and hold him in deep.

She was fucking Xena, warrior princess.

He caught a glimpse of rounded booty and black lace riding up butt cheeks before she quickly plonked her ass back on the couch.

His brain temporarily flatlined, but then they were off again, and Dex was determined to get her naked. Gaming wasn't instinctive to him. There hadn't been video games in his house growing up. Hell, there'd barely been enough money for food. He'd gotten into the scene late. A lot later than Harper, clearly, who took down another of his men after fifteen minutes of brilliant, methodical, relentless play.

Dex's hands trembled as he peeled his jeans down, a thrill of anticipation shooting through him. He was conscious of cool air relieving the building heat in his thighs and cooling his groin. Conscious of her head being level with the thick press of his erection against the fabric of his briefs.

Conscious of her deliberately averted gaze.

He wondered if she'd be so proper when he was completely exposed to her view.

Blood pounded thick and hot through his system. He could almost feel it surging through his neck and chest and groin.

As it happened, she lost the next man and her T-shirt came off. She didn't stand this time, just lifted it over her head to reveal a matching black lace bra before quickly restarting the game with absolutely no comment. Unfortunately Dex couldn't afford to take his eyes off the screen for even a second to check her out because he was damned if he was going to lose his last piece of clothing before she'd at least lost that bra.

It took another ten minutes of furious play for him to kill another of her guys. He was breathing hard by the time the shot hit its mark. From the mental exercise. From the thrill of the chase. From the high-octane sexual anticipation.

This time he did look. Wild horses couldn't have stopped him.

"You want some help with that?" he asked, as her hands slid around her back to the fastening of her bra.

"This would be a good time to do the gentlemanly thing and avert your eyes," she suggested, her voice husky.

"Are you kidding?" he murmured. "I've been fantasising about what's in that bra ever since the day of the overalls."

Dex swore he could see a splash of colour darken her cheekbones, despite the poor light.

"They look better *in* the bra."

"Oh, baby." Dex shook his head. "I can absolutely guarantee you they do *not*."

She hesitated for a beat or two then flicked the clasp open, letting the straps fall down her arms before she tossed the bra away.

His breath hissed out as her breasts swung free. She didn't try to hide herself but she didn't look at him either as he ogled them like some horny teenage boy salivating over his first girlie magazine. They were big and soft, the glow from the television accentuating the uptilt of two hard nipples, appearing mocha in the low light.

Saliva coated Dex's mouth as he remembered how good those nipples had felt against his tongue. Hell, he wanted to throw the controller down and devour every inch of them.

Every inch of *her*.

"Let's play," she said, still not looking in his direction.

Dex had barely gathered his wits when the game started again and within seconds his next man was dead. She whooped and turned a victorious smile on him, making an *L* on her forehead with her thumb and forefinger as she beamed at him.

She was magnificent, the state of her undress temporarily forgotten in her triumph.

He grinned at her. "I think you may just be the perfect woman."

"Oh?" She kicked up an eyebrow.

"Curvy," he said, his gaze drifting to her breasts then lower to her hips and belly and lower again to follow the line of her thigh, "*and* kick-ass. My two favourite traits."

She grinned at him. "That's game over for you, rugby."

"You're right." Dex stood, hooking his thumbs into the waistband of his Calvin's, restrictive against the urgent push of his erection.

"No," she said hurriedly, the controller clattering to the coffee table as she reached out to still him with a hand on his arm. Her breasts jiggled with the movement, and his dick bucked at the sight. "No need. The win is enough."

"Oh no," he shook his head. "You won fair and square. To the victor the spoils."

Chapter Six

Before she could utter another word to stop him, or draw breath to change her mind, Dex peeled his underwear off. He almost groaned as his cock sprang from the constriction of fabric. It felt so damn good to set his junk free, sticking out hard and potent in front of him like a goddamn divining rod sensing a nearby woman.

He glanced down at her, suddenly nervous at her reaction. Would she tell him to get dressed and get out? Or would she reach out and touch him?

To his relief, she didn't avert her eyes this time. On the contrary, she was looking her fill, her mouth slightly parted. Dex's balls contracted. Her head was about a foot from his cock, and all he could think about was her saying she should have gone down on her knees for him.

He ached to feel her mouth pushing down the length of him, the hot clamp of her lips, the light scrape of her teeth, and the hollow of her cheeks as she sucked.

"So, we're not doing the platonic thing, then?" she asked, dragging her gaze off his cock for a moment to meet his eyes.

Dex chuckled. "All my good intentions seem to disappear around you." That should be panicking him. Dex always meant what he said to women. And he never changed his mind.

Harper Nugent seemed to be the exception.

"I think you may just be the perfect man," she whispered.

Dex smiled. "Oh yeah?"

She nodded, her gaze lighting again on his dick. "Big." She flicked her gaze upward. "And kick-ass."

He chuckled, but then she wet her lips with her tongue and the laughter ended on a strangled groan.

"Bring those spoils over here," she said, crooking her finger at him.

Dex's heart punched like bullets into his rib cage, and his legs almost gave way as he willed them to move. One pace brought him level with her, and it was all he could do not to push her back against the couch and devour her.

"What do you want?" Her voice was husky as she slid her hands onto his thighs, and Dex shivered at her touch.

He shrugged. Just looking down at her like this, her face upturned, her long dark hair falling down her naked back, her breasts thrust out and tipped in a golden glow from the television, was driving him crazy. "They're your spoils."

She wet her lips again, and it took all Dex's willpower not to swoop down and crush his mouth on hers.

"I want to know."

Dex shook his head. She'd be shocked if she knew the things he wanted to do to her. "Trust me." He reached his hand out and pushed a lock of her hair behind her ear. "You don't."

She dug the pads of her fingers into his thighs and the sensation streaked straight to his balls, sizzling hot at the base of his spine. "Humour me."

Dex locked his gaze with hers. He could see fever glint

in their depths. The kind of fever that heated his blood and stirred deep in the muscles of his inner thighs.

She wanted to hear the words…

"I want to strip that underwear off you. I want to lay you flat and bury my head between your thighs and stay there until you forget the name of any other man who's ever gone down on you."

He trailed his fingers along her jaw, not trusting himself in this moment to not follow through on what he'd just described. His thumb rubbed at the full, soft crescent of her bottom lip.

"I want to kiss you until we both can't breathe. I want to push your gorgeous breasts together and thrust my cock between them until I come all over them. I want to look down and see your mouth around my dick."

Dex sucked in an uneven breath. He was dizzy with the images bombarding his mind, intoxicated by the possibilities, by the things he wanted to do to this woman. *With* this woman.

"I want to turn you upside down and inside out with wanting me. I want to bend you over the arm of this couch and fuck you until you're begging me to stop. Hell, I want to bend you over every goddamn piece of furniture in this place."

Dex stopped, the breath thick in the back of his throat, his mind swirling into an abyss of devolving scenarios. Ropes, paddles, wax encrusted nipples. *All that* Fifty Shades of Grey *shit.* He wasn't into pain—hers or his. But the way she was looking up at him, her pretty, wet lips parted and so very near, was fogging his brain with reckless lust.

"Well all right, then." It was gratifying to hear her voice was as husky as his. "How about we start with this one?" She moved swiftly, her mouth sliding down the length of his cock in one purposeful movement.

"*Fuuuck*," Dex groaned, grabbing for her shoulders as his knees threatened to buckle.

She withdrew, swirling her tongue around the head before plunging onto him again, her fingers digging into his thighs.

"*Yesss*," he hissed, his eyes shutting. "Fuck. Yes."

And she did it again and again, sure and slow and thorough, her mouth just the right amount of wet, applying just the right amount of suction.

She did it until he was dizzy with pleasure. Until the centre of his universe narrowed to the point where her lips met his dick, and all sensation burst from that point only, streaking heat and pleasure in waves up his torso, down his legs and driving it deep into his buttocks, wrapping silken fingers around the base of his spine and squeezing, sparking red-hot need all the way up to the base of his skull.

She moaned her own pleasure, her hands sliding around to the backs of his thighs, urging him closer, taking him deeper, and Dex groaned as the head of his cock hit the back of her throat.

"Harper," he murmured, his legs trembling and his glutes clenching as he prised his eyes open, looking down at her.

Her eyes fluttered open, and their gazes locked as she continued to work him. *Fuck.* He pushed the wavy curtain of her hair back. A hand clutched at his gut and squeezed hard. Dex hadn't seen anything more beautiful than her looking up at him, her bare breasts swaying as his cock slid deep into her mouth.

And he was hit with an overwhelming urge to be inside her—over her, on top of her. He wanted another part of her clamped around him as his building orgasm hit. He wanted to *kiss* her as he slid inside her body. He wanted to cover her mouth with his and mingle her cries with his own as they came.

God knew, her blowing him like this was tempting. He was about as turned on now as he'd ever been, and for damn sure he hoped that she'd do this again, but...not this time.

With supreme effort he pulled his dick out of her mouth,

taking a half step back in case he was tempted to just plunge it back in there again and to hell with it.

"Dex?" She blinked up at him, looking a little puzzled and confused, her mouth so damn wet, her lips dark and full from the sucking.

She looked lust drunk and needy. Wanton. Like a fucking goddess.

And *he'd* done that to her.

"Fuck," he whispered, his heartbeat galloping as emotion erupted in his chest and fogged his senses. He swooped down to claim her mouth. To taste it. To lick it. To devour every swollen millimetre of it. His fingers ploughed deep into her hair, and she moaned against his lips as he kissed her harder, hyperextending her neck in his greedy demand for more.

"Lay back," he panted, breaking away finally.

"Condom?" She was panting, too.

He nodded. "In my wallet. I'll get it. You…" He reached down and pinged the side seam of her underwear against the flesh of her hip. "Get out of those."

Dex turned away, groping for his jeans on the floor, the sounds of Harper squirming around on the couch behind messing with his fine motor control. He located his wallet quickly and grabbed a condom. The foil packet slipped out of his hands twice, and he cursed it under his breath.

In rugby, Dex was known *worldwide* for his sure, safe hands. Someone threw him a ball and he never let go of it — not even in rainy conditions that made grip nigh on impossible. But right now — as he dropped the condom for the third time — a small square foil packet was absolutely defeating him.

He steadied himself and took a slow deep breath, trying to still the fine tremble of his hands and clear some of the sticky fog of desire from his brain.

It worked. He grabbed hold of the condom, ripped it

open, and had himself sheathed in seconds. Which was just as well because when he turned back to the couch, what he saw just about caused him to lose his load on the spot—a buck naked Harper on her knees, leaning over the high arm of the couch on bent elbows, heavy breasts swinging free. The glow from the television accentuated her tan, the river of hair flowing down her back, and the round globes of her ass pushed enticingly in his direction.

She was looking over her shoulder at him. "Is this okay?"

Dex blinked. *Okay?* She couldn't have been any more okay had she been dipped in marshmallow and rolled in coconut.

"Uhh…" At least Dex hoped it came out as that, instead of the *uhmphgng* it had sounded like in his head.

"Well?" Harper smiled, arching her back as she angled herself up onto the palms of her hands and wiggled her ass. "Are you bringing your spoils over here, or am I going to have to start without you?"

That pulled Dex out of his inertia and had him striding the two paces to the couch. "As tempting as it is to stand here and watch you getting off"—he sunk a knee down on the sofa's edge—"I need to be inside you more."

The front of his thigh fit along the back of hers as Dex stroked a hand up the furrow of her spine. She shivered as he pushed her hair aside and it slid over the shoulder closest to the couch.

"You're beautiful," he murmured, brushing his mouth up the path his hand had just taken, from the small of her back to the first notch of her nape. Goose bumps buzzed his lips, and she moaned long and low when he swiped his tongue up the side of her neck.

"You make me feel beautiful," she gasped, reaching both hands behind her to plough into the back of his hair and anchor his front to her back.

Her chest opened up and her breasts thrust out enticingly as his other knee hit the couch. Their thighs nestled together as the rock hard length of his cock found the cleft of her buttocks. Dex ground against her as he slid both his hands up her stomach and over her ribs to claim her breasts.

"Fuck, I love these," he groaned in her ear, still grinding as he squeezed the lush flesh in his hands and pincered the hard peaks of her nipples between thumb and forefinger. She bucked and cried out, and he taunted them some more just to hear the noises she made—the breathy pants, the whimpery moans—and know that it was he who caused them.

"Dex...please," she begged on a hoarse moan, her hips rotating in an agitated rhythm to the slow grind of his cock.

She sounded as desperate as he felt.

"Shhh," he soothed, his hands falling from her breasts and feathering down her body as he eased away from her. Her hands fell from his hair as his trailed to her back, urging her gently down over the arm of the couch again, his thighs bracketing hers. She went eagerly, falling onto her elbows as if she could no longer keep herself upright.

God, she was magnificent. Her rich brown hair tumbling over the straight plains of back, the hourglass curve of her waist flaring out to the buxom line of her hips, her ass jammed into the cradle of his pelvis and *perfectly* splayed.

Her tiny waist leading to the rounded flesh of her butt was dizzying. He grabbed a cheek in both hands and kneaded.

Vigorously.

The arch of her back, her answering moan almost brought him undone.

"I want to..." Dex sucked in a breath. God, he didn't know where to start. He vibrated from toes to scalp with the need to *possess*, his heart galloping in his chest. He wanted to kiss it, lick it. *Bite it.* He wanted to grip it hard as he hammered into her. He wanted to feel it move and clench with every thrust and slam of his body.

He shifted slightly to rub his cock up and down the slick folds of her sex. She gasped this time, rotating her hips.

"Yes, yes. *Please, Dex*. God, yes."

The urgency in her voice, the throbbing in his groin, the roaring in his blood reached a crescendo that could not be denied, and Dex swiftly notched himself at her entrance and thrust.

Her head reared back, and they both cried out as he pushed high and hard inside her. Neither moved for long moments. Dex just breathed, absorbing the tumble of sensations before primal instinct kicked in demanding more.

"Christ," he murmured, sagging against her back and planting kisses down her neck. He wondered if she could feel the frantic punch of his heart. "You feel good."

"You feel *big*," she panted, amusement lacing her voice as she flexed her pelvis a little.

"Jesus." He gripped her hips, holding her tight against him as her internal muscles massaged his cock. "Do that again."

She laughed and undulated muscles up and down the length of him again. "Yoga," she said. "Great for the pelvic floor."

He laughed. "You want to know what else is good for the pelvic floor? Orgasms." And he withdrew his cock almost all the way before sliding in again.

"More fun than yoga," Harper moaned as she pushed back, inviting him in deeper.

Dex followed. He couldn't not. And then there was no more talking as the spark caught and the rhythm of their bodies took over. Instead, he tuned into the saw of his breath and the wash of blood through his ears and the unbearable ache in his balls. Into the incoherent noises falling from her mouth and the delicious tightness of her and the glorious shift and clench of her ass with each flex of his hips.

But soon it wasn't enough. He needed to touch her, all over. He needed more skin on skin. He needed his mouth on hers. Not missing a beat, he slid his hands from her hips around to her belly and then up—up her stomach, over her ribs, urging her against him as he thrust in and out, rocking her body with each jerk of his hips.

Finally his hands found her swaying breasts, and she gasped as he cupped them. "Yes," she moaned as his fingers taunted the nipples to stiff points.

Dex nuzzled her hair and murmured, "Kiss me," into her ear.

Her response was instantaneous. She turned her head, her lips blindly seeking his. There was nothing glamorous about the kiss. It was breathy and sloppy and noisy, more passion than finesse, but it was like a hit of speed tripping through his blood, rippling pleasure through his thighs and buttocks and belly, their heads twisting greedily in time to the wild buck of his hips.

Dex broke off, groaning "Harper," low in her ear, her nipples harder than he'd ever felt them before. "You're making me come. Want to come with me?"

She moaned, "*God yes,*" her hand loosening its grip on his thigh to slide between her legs.

"*No.*" Dex relinquished a breast to pull her hand away, his fingers taking the place of hers. "*I* want to."

She gasped, and her body trembled against him as he found the hard little pearl between her legs. "God, you're wet," he whispered as he rubbed in time with his own strokes, burying himself inside her to the hilt with each thrust.

"Dex," she moaned, turning her head toward him again. There was so much in that desperate little tremble in her voice that he understood. Need. And ache. And want.

Her lips found his, and he met the demand in her kiss. Kept pace with it, kissing her long and deep and wet. The angle was awkward for both of them but it didn't matter. All that mattered was his mouth on hers, his cock moving inside her, his fingers moving outside her.

The feel of her body against his.

The combined beat of their hearts, and the frantic pull of their breathing.

It didn't take long for the pleasure to overtake them. They came together in a wild, reckless, sweaty mess. Dex did his best to hold her as she splintered apart, falling against the arm of the couch, following her down, clutching her to him, pumping his hips as he, too, splintered, riding the spiral through a kaleidoscope sky for as long as it lasted. He clung to her as she rode it with him, thankful for the solid furniture beneath his knees keeping their bodies earthbound as their minds twirled together on some astral plane somewhere.

She called out his name and he called out hers as they were dumped out the other end in a gasping heap, collapsing against each other, barely able to move, to breathe, to *think*.

All he could do was just…exist, just *be*…in a state of utter content.

Deep down in his bones content. The type of content that only came from beating the All Blacks or a truly good orgasm.

Both of them had been awfully frickin' rare.

Hopefully not anymore.

• • •

"You know what this poker game needs?"

There were general groans around the table. Linc said the same thing every poker night.

"Let me guess," Bodie Webb chimed in sarcastically as he dealt out six hands. "Is it women?"

Linc raised his beer bottle. "You got it, Spidey."

"No women," Tanner Stone growled.

It was the skipper's one rule. For the last couple of years, the game had been held at Tanner's luxurious apartment situated at the prestigious Finger Wharf on Sydney Harbour, but since he'd hooked up with his high school girlfriend and now *shacked up* with her, they'd moved the show to Dex's place.

According to Tanner, poker night needed a bachelor pad, and his place no longer qualified. A point proven by the fact that at the present time, Matilda and some of the other WAGS, along with Valerie King, the coach's daughter, were drinking wine on his balcony at Finger Wharf.

Dex had volunteered his digs as an alternative. He owned an apartment near Henley Stadium, the Smoke's home ground. It was in a gated community in an exclusive area with its own courtyard and a ten-minute drive to the stadium. It wasn't Sydney Harbour. But it was no Perry Hill, either.

"I'm just sayin'," Linc continued, "there are very few scenarios that cannot be improved with some female company."

Ryder Davis, his big, round belt buckle glinting in the downlights, looked out from under the brim of his Akubra and raised his beer to Linc. "That's what Brooks and Dunn reckon anyway." Which just went to show you could take the boy out of the country but not the country out of the boy.

"Well, I don't know who they are." Linc grinned, taking a swig of his beer, "but I like 'em."

"Jesus, Linc," Ryder bitched. "That's like saying you don't know who…" He cast around, obviously lost for a suitable comparison.

"Simon and Garfunkel," Donovan Bane, who was taking his seat after a visit to the bathroom, offered helpfully.

"Thank you. Who Simon and Garfunkel are."

Linc frowned. "Who the fuck are Simon and Garfunkel?"

"Bloody hell," Bodie groaned as the others laughed.

"Just as well you can kick a ball. What the hell do you talk to women about?"

"Who says we talk about anything?"

Donovan shook his head. "One day some woman is going to do a number on you, and I hope I'm around to see it."

"Not a chance, Dono." Linc shook his head cockily. "Too many chicks. Not enough time. Why settle for just one?"

"Maybe we should ask the boss?" Donovan suggested, reaching for his sixth slice of pizza. The front-rower was a hard guy to fill up. At six foot three he was, in part thanks to his Maori heritage, built like a brick shithouse.

Everyone glanced at Tanner, who gave a nonchalant shrug but couldn't hide the start of a goofy grin. His mates gave him absolute hell for it, drumming on the table and grunting "Woo, woo, woo," like a bunch of wild gorillas.

"Okay, okay," Tanner griped good-naturedly, picking up his hand now Donovan was back. "Are we playing fucking poker or you want to sit around and knit or something?"

Everyone followed suit, and there was quiet for long moments as they checked out their hands. "Speaking of chicks," Linc said, breaking the silence and glancing over the top of his cards at Dex. "How's things with Chuck's sister?"

Dex had been having a good night. He'd heaped plenty of crap on his mates while avoiding the same fate, and he was winning. Glancing at his pathetic hand and the five pairs of eyes now trained quizzically on him, he figured he'd just run shit out of luck.

"Nuthin' to tell," he remarked casually as he threw four cards down, retaining his ace.

Nothing he wanted to tell them anyway.

Nothing he wanted to think about right now, given how he'd crept out of her bed at dawn and left without saying good-bye.

He'd fallen asleep.

Dexter Blake *did not* fall asleep with a woman. He didn't spend the night. He was still trying to wrap his head around that one. And the fact she hadn't contacted him…

In his experience, women always tried to push him for more.

"I'll take four," he said to Ryder.

"You go on that date?" Tanner asked.

"Yep."

"How was it?" he pushed.

Dex shot his friend and captain a you-have-to-be-shitting-me look. "We playing fucking poker or knitting?"

Tanner whistled long through his teeth and shook his head in faux seriousness. "That good, huh?"

"Sure as shit doesn't sound like he got laid, does it?" Linc added.

Bodie nodded. "Totally struck out," he agreed.

"She do that painting?" Donovan asked, lifting his chin toward the kitchen.

Dex had glued some magnetic strips to the back of the canvas frame and slapped it on the side of his fridge. He'd forgotten about it being there. "Yep."

Four pairs of eyes swivelled to the painting. Linc got up— *of course he did*—to inspect it closer. He plucked it off the fridge and brought it back to the table. "That's some girly-assed goalposts," he said as he passed it around.

Dex felt unaccountably twitchy at the painting being pawed by a bunch of blokes who wouldn't know a work of art from their elbows.

"Looks like those murals we saw at the kids hospital last week," Bodie said when it got to him. "Hey, wait a minute…" He glanced at Dex. "This is her signature, too." He pointed at where Harper had signed it. "I remember that little heart instead of the a."

Dex wondered how long it would take Linc's filthy mind

to connect the dots.

Not long, as it turned out.

"*Aha*," he crowed, grinning around his beer bottle as he took a triumphant swig. "So *that's* where you disappeared to the other day."

"And came back with a mysteriously wet jersey," Tanner added.

Dex glared at his friend. "The *tap* over sprayed."

Everyone laughed. "*Something* over sprayed," Linc said. "It's usually what happens when you live like a monk. Massive sperm pressure, man, I'm telling you, it'll kill you."

"And what would *you* know about MSP, Linc?" Donovan quipped.

"It's *platonic*," Dex growled, wanting to put an end to the conversation for once and for all.

"Sure it is." Tanner grinned. "If platonic means ripping one off with Chuckie's sister in a hospital full of sick kids."

Dex flipped him the bird. "Bite me."

"Methinks he doth protest too much," Donovan mused.

Linc frowned. "He doth wha?"

Donovan rolled his eyes. "It's *Shakespeare*, dickhead."

The guys laughed, but Dex was done with them discussing him and Harper. "For Chrissakes, are we playing or not?" he demanded then glared at Ryder. "I need four fucking cards."

Everyone laughed, but Ryder dealt, and the game got back on track.

Chapter Seven

Two days later, Harper was done with waiting. "That's it," she said to Em, "I'm texting him."

She hadn't contacted Dex before now because she didn't want to freak him out any more if he was already freaked out enough.

Em, who was still in full-on wallow mode, practically inhaling an entire two-litre tub of rocky road ice cream before Harper's eyes, snatched the phone from Harper's fingers. "No."

She was surprisingly quick for someone with only one unoccupied hand, who looked like she survived on thin air. That'd be the sixty billion ice-cream calories she was currently consuming.

She shoved the phone in her back pocket. "Absolutely not."

"It's just one text."

Harper had been disappointed to wake Monday morning and find the bed empty, but not surprised. Dex had been upfront concerning his attitude toward dating and relationships, and there wasn't anything between them. Aside from some truly awesome sex.

Which had, admittedly, complicated things somewhat.

But only if they let it.

She just hoped his silence wasn't because he was checking himself into a witness protection program somewhere.

"That's not the way this works," Em insisted. "Treat them mean, keep them keen."

Harper blinked. Em had *never* treated a man mean in her entire existence. She was the very definition of a pushover and men knew it.

"You were the one who said I should go out with him to get up Chuck's nose."

"That's because I was drunk. And now I'm sober, and as your friend, I am duty bound to inform you that all men are bastards."

Em was still shitty on men in general and determined to concentrate on her career as a high school science teacher instead.

Knowing Em like she did, Harper thought that'd probably only last to next week.

"You know we're talking about *my* situation now, right?"

"It applies to *any* situation," Em said.

Harper doubted it. Considering she'd already blown the whole treating-him-mean thing by getting down and dirty with him two out of the three times they'd met, it was a little hard to go back.

"We're not a *thing*," she insisted. "That's not what we're doing. I just want to check he's not freaking out."

"He *should* be freaking out," Em said around a mouthful of ice cream, jabbing her spoon in Harper's direction. Harper had her own spoon, not that she was getting much of the sweet treat that Em was zealously hoovering up. "He slept with you and snuck out like a bloody thief in the night. I *hate* it when men do that."

Harper shrugged. "I don't care about that."

"Well, *I* care." More spoon jabbing. "He better not show his face around me or I'll…"

She stopped and inspected the ice cream like it might suggest a suitable punishment. "Send him to the principal?" Harper ventured.

"Ha." Em glanced at her, face stern. "You are so funny." Then she returned her attention to the ice cream, hunching over it further.

"Would you like me to leave you two alone?"

Em looked up apologetically. "Sorry," she grimaced. "I can't seem to stop."

Harper sighed, placing her spoon down. "Don't worry about it." She patted Em's hand. "It'll just go to my ass anyway. And I have to go pick up Jace and Tabby from their gym class."

Em nodded and handed over Harper's phone. "I love you. Stay strong."

Harper took it, nodding assuredly, with absolutely no intention of listening to a woman high on sugar and man-hate.

No matter how much she loved the nutter.

She waited till she got to the car before she texted. It took her another ten minutes to compose, edit, delete, recompose, and edit again before she settled on what she wanted to convey. That she wasn't pissed about waking up alone. That she was up for some casual fun. That she didn't expect anything from him.

Which was *all* true.

Sure, she didn't normally do this kind of thing, but why not? Plenty of women did. And she was young and alive. If the sudden death of two parents had taught her nothing else, it was that everything could be over in the blink of an eye.

She read over the text one last time.

In overalls. Will be home in one hour. Need a hand with my zip if you're around.

She hit send quickly, before she could change her mind, and then started the car.

Harper pulled into her townhouse complex one hour and ten minutes later. Dex hadn't replied, and she didn't know what that meant. Had she gotten the tone all wrong? Had she overstepped the mark? Had it freaked him out even more, and he was too chicken shit to tell her he didn't want anything to do with her?

Or maybe…he was just busy and hadn't checked his phone yet.

Thoughts churning wildly, she slowed her car down to ten, obeying the speed limit in the complex as she navigated to the driveway that serviced the block of four townhouses where hers was situated. A car was parked outside in one of the guest spaces. It belonged to Dex. She'd seen it the night of the wine and paint party. And even if she hadn't, the rugby stickers on the bumper would have given it away.

RUGBY PLAYERS DO IT WITH GRUNT was her favourite.

The car was empty, so he must be waiting for her inside the hallway to her apartment. That was a good sign, right? Her heart thumped hard in her chest for a beat or two before accelerating at a lighter, quicker pace.

There was only one way to find out…

Harper garaged her car quickly, her hand unsteady as she reached to open the door. She paused with her fingers around the handle, making a snap decision. Quickly she unzipped her overalls, slid her hands around the back and unhooked her bra. Pulling the straps down her arms and out the end of the overalls, she whipped the bra off and tossed it on the backseat before zipping up again.

She pulled her hair out of its ponytail, too, and gave it a quick shake, scrunching the natural waves to give them some volume.

Maybe he was here to tell her he'd changed his mind about their arrangement. But if he wasn't? Why not be prepared…

Dex was lounging against her door, his phone in hand, when Harper stepped into the corridor that fronted all four townhouses. She shut the door that led from her garage behind her and headed in his direction, anticipation tingling between her legs.

She'd been hoping for round four when she'd woken Monday morning, and had been frustrated to find that wasn't going to happen.

She'd been fantasising about it ever since.

He straightened as she approached, slipping his phone into his pocket. "Wow," she said, her gaze devouring the way the fabric of his dark suit outlined his shoulders and pulled taut across his thighs. His hair had been carelessly ruffled with some kind of gel into a sexy-messy combo, and he was cleanly shaven.

"You didn't have to dress."

The man looked hot in his jersey, sexy as hell in a pair of jeans, and goddamn mouth-watering in nothing but his tan.

In a business suit? He looked utterly fuckable.

As she pulled up in front of him, Harper had to grind her heels into the floor to stop herself from climbing up his body. She couldn't believe she had carnal knowledge of every delicious inch of what lay under that suit.

She smiled, searching his face for any hint of hesitance or withdrawal. She'd seen it in the faces of enough guys over the years to know the signs. All she found was a slow grin and eyes that had already locked onto her zip like a heat-seeking missile.

"Oh yes," he said, glancing dismissively at his suit. "I have an official rugby thing to go to, so…"

Harper felt a hot spike of disappointment that he was going out. Without her. Which was completely *insane*. Whatever he did, wherever he went, was no business of hers—that wasn't the kind of dating they were doing.

Besides, he probably already had a date. One of those women the WAGS liked to set him up with.

Skinny women.

"But…" He smiled at her as he shoved his hands in his pockets. The action parted his jacket below the buttons, revealing the tight pull of his trousers across the tops of his thighs, and Harper's knees weakened. "I couldn't leave you here wrestling with your zipper all alone, now could I?"

She shook her head. "Absolutely not."

"I figured I could offer my services, at the very least."

"That's very gentlemanly of you."

He laid a hand across his chest. "But of course. That's why I play rugby."

Harper laughed. "Oh really?"

"Well, that's why *I* do. I'm pretty sure guys like Lincoln Quinn only play it to get laid."

"Oh, I don't know," she teased. "That seems to be working out for you quite well at the moment."

His gaze dropped to her mouth, and Harper's breath hitched. "I can't complain."

They stood staring at each other for long moments, Harper trying not to grin like a goofball at Dex.

"You want me to give you a hand with that thing out here," he asked, finally breaking their strange inertia. "Or you want to take this inside?"

Harper gave herself a mental shake. *Pull yourself together woman.* "Sure." She stepped around him and shoved her key in the door, throwing "Come in," over her shoulder as she strode ahead of him, determined to act cool if it killed her.

Act nonchalant.

Like she had hot rugby players help her with her zip every day of the week. Twice on Sunday.

"You want a drink?" She threw her handbag on the central island countertop as she headed straight for the fridge, pulling it open. "I have some beer. There's some coke, too," she mused, bending slightly to paw through an array of half eaten food in some sudden manic nervousness. "Although, I think it's diet. Or I can do a coffee."

She straightened and looked over her shoulder. He was leaning casually against the island, the two buttons of his jacket undone, clearly checking out her ass. Heated awareness of him darted seductively from one side of her pelvis to the other, and her mouth turned as dry as day old toast.

"Or tea," she ended lamely. Christ…next she'd be going all *Notting Hill* on him and offering him some bloody apricots in honey.

He shook his head as he lifted his gaze to her face. "I don't want a drink."

Good for him. She sure as hell could do with one. A big one. A vat, preferably, of something dangerously alcoholic that would still the frantic pulse hammering between her legs.

"I wanted to say something…"

"Oh?" Harper hoped she sounded nonchalant.

"About Sunday night."

"*Oh.*"

"I'm sorry I left the way I did," he apologised, shoving his hands back in his pockets. "Without waking you. I don't usually stay the…"

He broke off, obviously deciding against that choice of words before boldly ploughing on.

"I mean, I don't usually fall asleep…after. Like that. And

I guess I panicked a little because you're the first woman I've felt really comfortable around. You don't expect me to be *on* around you, to be the rugby star, and I was really petrified I'd probably blown that. But I still should have woken you or left a note or something. I wasn't thinking. I just needed to get out in case you woke and thought…"

He broke off again, a deep crease furrowing between his eyebrows as he shoved a hand through his hair, messing up the already artfully messy style. She loved that he felt comfortable around her. That she put him at ease. She supposed some women would consider that an insult to their femininity, but the truth was she felt comfortable around him, too.

Appreciated.

Secure in his desire for her, and not self-conscious as she so often was around men.

Harper smiled at his obvious discomfiture, and quirked an eyebrow. "In case I thought that you staying the night was a sign of your undying love and fidelity and you were about to pledge me your troth?"

He gave a short laugh, thick with irony, as he shifted uncomfortably. "Something like that." He inspected the ground for a moment before he raised his gaze to her again, full of earnest intent. "I really like you, but I really, *really* need to concentrate on rugby at the moment."

Wow. The guy had obviously twisted himself in knots over this. "It's okay, Dex," Harper said, shutting the fridge door and walking toward him, halting a couple of metres away. "I understand. And you don't owe me any explanations. Stay the night, don't stay the night. I'm not going to read *anything* into it, okay? If you want to hang out, then I'm around. *Your* call. I'm not going to boil your pet bunny or tell Facebook you have a small dick, I promise."

"Good to know." He laughed, and the crease between his eyebrows ironed out.

Harper sucked in a breath as it transformed his face, and he went from earnest and serious back to utterly fuckable again. Her nipples, bare beneath the overalls, brushed against the material, scrunching into tight points. Awareness tickled low and deep as if he had swiped his tongue along the sensitive skin that sloped from her hip bone to groin.

Oestrogen fogged her brain with primal demands.

"So," she said, taking a step closer, tugging the tab he'd been periodically eyeing down with a loud *zzzzip*.

Dex stilled as his gaze zeroed in on her chest. "*Holy. Fuck.*"

Harper wasn't sure how much the fabric gaped or how much Dex could see but she could feel the touch of cool air on the centre of her chest, and the intensity of his stare spoke volumes.

"I believe you were going to help me with this?"

He swallowed as he dragged his gaze north. "Your zipper seems more than fine to me."

"You got me." Harper shrugged knowing the motion would cause the fabric to gape even more. "I used it to shamelessly lure you here."

"You're so bad." He grinned. "I don't know *how* you live with yourself."

"You're right," she murmured, taking the last two steps toward him slowly, until the front of her body was a whisker from the front of his. Their level gazes locked. "I may need to be punished."

His pupils dilated as Harper's ears filled with his unsteady breath and the ring of her own heartbeat. Her nostrils filled with the intoxicating accents of some posh cologne. Heat poured into her belly and streaked down her thighs.

He kissed her then. Hard and hot. His smell, his taste, the harsh, feral suck of his breath, the pure *urgency* of his mouth, flamed through her. His tongue thrust into her mouth as his hands invaded her gaping overalls, sliding onto her waist, yanking her body against his before turning them, switching positions, trapping her between him and the island bench.

"I want to fuck you," he muttered, grinding the steely hardness of his cock between her legs as his mouth left hers, nipping and sucking a trail of kisses down her neck.

Harper moaned as she ground back, her eyes squeezing shut at the wild clamp of her internal muscles. *God. Yes.* If this was the way he punished her, then she was going to be bad a lot more often.

His mouth savaged lower, the sheer force of his passion bending her back against the bench, his tongue tracing over her collarbones and lower, his hands pushing at the opening of the overalls, exposing her breasts, groaning at the sight of them, cupping them, kneading them, his fingers squeezing the taut, tight nipples until she cried out at the twin sensations of pleasure-pain before lowering his head to soothe them with the hot lick of his tongue.

Harper closed her eyes and buried her hands in his hair, arching her back shamelessly as the scrape of his teeth and the deliciously brutal suction of his mouth rendered her incapable of coherent thought.

Too soon he broke away, and she cried out a weak protest, but he simply moved north again, his hands urging her into a more upright position, before sliding to the backs of her thighs as he whispered a ragged "Up," in her ear, lifting her onto the bench as if she weighed nothing at all.

She clutched his shoulders as he seated her and then thanked the kitchen gods that her high benches were the exact level required to bring the big, beautiful bulge in his trousers directly in contact with the big, bitching ache between her legs.

She locked her legs around his waist and moaned as he rocked into her, claiming her mouth with the same mastery as before—deep and hard. But Harper was done with the dry humping. Done with clothes. She needed to touch him. To feel his cock in her hand. Feel it inside her.

She *needed* that intimate connection with him so damn much that nothing else mattered.

Still kissing him, she pushed frantically at his jacket, desperate to get closer to him. She made a triumphant sound in the back of her throat as it fell off his arms, and she greedily smoothed her hands across the breadth of his pecs, over the roundness of his shoulders, and then down his back.

Her hands landed on his ass and she pulled him in tighter, rocking him closer.

He groaned, breaking the kiss, his forehead pressing into hers. "God, woman, you make me see stars."

There was a bulge in his back pocket and she yanked out his wallet, opening it without asking, finding what she wanted. "Condom," she said, slapping it against his chest.

The wallet fell to the benchtop as she reached for his belt buckle, her fingers making surprisingly short work of both it and his fly, considering how crazily they trembled.

As crazy as the wild clatter of her heart.

He groaned, their foreheads still together, when Harper breached the waistband of his underwear and pulled out his erection, stiff and eager, the head plump between the press of their bodies.

"*Jesus,*" he muttered. "That's so damn good it hurts."

"Feels pretty damn good to me, too," she murmured, loving the silk and the steel of it as she closed her fist around him, sliding up and down a couple of times. "*Condom,*" she panted.

"Lie back," he said as he ripped at the foil packet with his teeth.

Harper didn't have to be asked twice, lowering back onto her elbows so she could watch him sheath himself, then catching the flare of his gaze as he glanced at her once he was done. He was looking at her as if he was a sugar addict and she was his own personal lolly shop.

He slid both hands up her torso, pushing her gently all the way back, as he palmed her breasts and squeezed. "God, you're beautiful," he said on a ragged breath, his hands smoothing down her body again.

So used to her love-hate relationship with her body, Harper realised that when Dex told her she was beautiful like that, with a note of reverence in his voice that almost made her cry, she actually believed him.

He shook his head as fingers brushed the lace edge of her purple satin underwear. "I don't know if I thought this through properly," he said, tracing down the two vertical lines of black ribbon decorating the front of her full-figured brief. "I should have ditched your clothes before I put you on the counter."

Harper closed her eyes to clear the sexual fog as his fingers continued down, brushing closer and closer to her aching sex. Thank God the baggy overalls were long in the crotch, giving them plenty of room to manoeuvre.

His thumb whispered over the satiny fabric between her legs, already damp from their making out, and she bit down on her lip. "Just push it aside," she urged, her voice all deep and growly, too far-gone to worry about logistics. Then she clamped her legs around his hips, her strong solid calves anchoring tight against the taut globes of his ass, and rubbed against him.

He groaned, yanking the fabric aside as she'd suggested, guiding himself through slick folds to her entrance, and thrust home. Harper gasped as it slammed like a shock wave through her body, rolling up from where they were joined to her throat, finding an outlet through a cry that exploded from her chest.

"Yes," she moaned, eyes shut tight, feeling the burn and tingle of his possession, blindsided by the completeness of it.

His hands clamped on her hips as he pulled out and thrust back in again. She was vaguely aware of the heavy bounce of her bare breasts as he rocked in and out of her one more time.

"God, I wish you could see yourself," Dex murmured, and Harper opened her eyes to find his glittering green gaze locked on her chest, following the motion of her breasts with every thrust of his hips. "You look incredible."

Harper arched her back and was rewarded with the flaring of his nostrils and the quickening of his breath. "Yes," Dex groaned, plunging in and out, harder and harder, watching intently as each shove jarred through her torso, jolting through her breasts with the convulsive force of an electric shock.

She was watching him intently, too. She couldn't look away from the feral lust on his face—the cording of his neck muscles, the tight clamp of his jaw, the baring of his teeth. It fed the heat building in her thighs and buttocks and belly. It stoked the fever raging out of control between her legs.

She'd never been so freaking turned on in her life.

She couldn't breathe or think or move. Only feel. The rigid clamp of his fingers on her hips, the cold press of the stone bench against her shoulder blades, and the deep, hard shove of him driving her closer and closer to nirvana.

Nearer and nearer.

When it happened, it happened fast, the tumult building in seconds, everything pulling taut inside her, wrenching a cry from her throat.

"*Dex!*"

"I'm here, baby," he panted, his voice ragged and strangled as he hammered in and out, everything a blur as the world disintegrated around her into a sticky quagmire of pleasure.

Suddenly, his head fell back on his neck and he let out a long guttural bellow as he joined her there, bucking wildly, emptying everything he had, giving it all until there was nothing left and he collapsed on top of her.

"Christ," he gasped, his head on her still heaving chest.

Harper automatically cradled him there, holding him close, her fingers twined in his hair as the mad synchronicity of their pulses and the unevenness of their breathing eventually slowed and settled. He lifted his head, propping his chin between her breasts, and she prised her eyes open, fighting the pull of postcoital drowsiness.

"My name on your lips as you come is the sexiest thing I've ever heard."

Her heart skipped a beat both at the sincerity of and the rough burr to his voice. Damned if the man didn't say the nicest things. She needed to watch herself around him—he was just too damn good for her ego.

He gathered her close and pulled her into a sitting position, his forehead pressing lightly against hers as he cast a last lingering look down at her breasts before pulling the sides of her overalls together and stepping back a pace.

"Bin under the sink," she said.

He nodded and turned to get rid of the condom. She watched him, liking the way his shoulders sat snug against the seams of his shirt as he reached for a paper towel, and the way his trousers cupped his ass like little elves had sewn it with threads of awesome.

Hell, she liked every single thing about this guy.

She zipped up before he headed back, all tucked in and immaculate again, picking his jacket up off the floor as he walked toward her. He placed it beside her before settling between her legs, sliding his hands up her thighs and onto her waist then kissing her thoroughly.

"Mmm," she murmured, her head spinning when they finally came up for air, his lips trekking to her ear. "What time does your thing start?"

He nuzzled her temple. "Fifteen minutes ago."

Harper straightened. "What? Oh my God!" She laughed as she pushed a hand against his chest. "Why didn't you tell me?"

"And miss out on *that*?" he asked, his voice low, tinged with laughter. "Are you crazy?"

Harper was beginning to think she very well may be. She picked up his jacket and shoved it at him. "Go."

"I will," he leaned toward her again. "In a second."

"No," she laughed, shoving harder. "Now."

"Okay, okay." He grabbed his jacket and shrugged into it. "You want to do something Sunday arvo?"

Harper nodded, her heart doing a merry little tap dance in her chest. She hadn't expected him to set another date with her right now. They hadn't discussed logistics, but she'd assumed they were going to be sporadic. She was inordinately pleased that he was lining something up again so quickly.

"Yes." But then she remembered she was busy and her hopes fell. "Oh no, wait…I can't. The twins are coming around on Sunday for movie afternoon."

"Okay," he nodded, roughly finger combing his hair. "Sounds good to me."

She frowned. "Oh. You want to…come over and watch a couple of movies with two eleven-year-olds?"

"And you." He smiled. "You're going to be here, too, right?"

Harper smiled back. "Yes…I'll be here, too."

"Cool. Sounds like fun. If it's okay by you?"

Stunned, it was a second or two before Harper bobbed her head wildly in the affirmative. "Of course. Sure."

Her devotion to her siblings had been the angst in one too many relationships. Often unable to go on dates because it clashed with her commitment to the twins, or having to cancel dates at the last minute due to one of the many unforeseen scenarios that could develop when children were involved, had caused more than one guy to walk away.

"Oh, hang on." He narrowed his eyes at her. "What movie? It's not some chick flick, is it?"

She rolled her eyes. "Star Wars, *of course*. We've been working our way through them all."

"Oh my God." He grinned as he moved quickly between her legs again. "You *are* the perfect woman. Curvy and kick-ass with *excellent* taste in movies."

He smacked a brief, hard kiss on her mouth. It lasted for only a few seconds but still managed to leave her woozy and breathless. "See you on Sunday," he said before stepping away and striding out of her house.

Harper happy-sighed as the door clicked shut after him.

She had excellent taste in men, too.

Chapter Eight

"How long do you think is reasonable to ask a guy to wait before you put out?"

Em was moving forward in her determination not to be a doormat with men anymore.

Harper gave her an A for effort but she'd been Em's shoulder to cry on too many times to believe that her friend wouldn't revert to type the next time a guy flashed her a *hey baby* smile.

She gave it a month, tops.

"If a guy's going to dump you because you won't put out, then he shouldn't be given the time of day," Harper said. It dodged the question, but it wasn't a subject she felt she had any authority on, given that she'd slept with Dex on their second date.

"Of course." Em nodded, her curls bouncing in Harper's peripheral vision. She had put out too many times for guys who'd been too impatient and too disrespectful to wait. A childhood spent with an emotionally distant father had left Harper's bestie starved of affection and unwilling to deny it when it did come her way.

Harper would have ordinarily taken the time to reinforce the point but her gaze was glued to the television, where a bunch of big, sweaty guys were running around playing rugby. Catching the occasional glimpse of Dex was worth the frequent glimpses of her stepbrother reporting, all smug and pretty from the sidelines.

It was almost halftime, and the Smoke were behind by three.

The play stopped as the ref blew his whistle and the camera zoomed in on Dex, who'd been crunched beneath two burly blokes from the opposing team. Ordinarily, three buff guys piled on top of each other would be quite the titillating sight, but it wasn't that kind of man-wich.

Harper winced as Dex staggered to his feet, blood pouring from a gash in his forehead. She wasn't too worried; she knew even the tiniest of head wounds could bleed impressively.

The ref and a few of the Smoke players gathered around as the two opposition players tried to talk their way out of a penalty. A couple of guys ran on from the sidelines to Dex's side. One was toting a small bag and wearing gloves, with MEDIC printed on the back of his Sydney Smoke shirt. The other was a kid with Down Syndrome, who looked about fifteen, carrying two bottles of water.

Dex held his hand out for some water and squirted it into his mouth in a long stream, his head tilted at an awkward angle to allow the medic to inspect the wound. He drank greedily. The medic said something and stood back a little as Dex squirted more water over the wound. Diluted blood ran down his face as the medic stepped back in, applying a gauze pad to the injury.

Dex gave the water back to the kid, smiling at him and giving him a fist bump. The kid beamed at Dex, and Harper's lungs suddenly felt too big for her chest cavity.

"Oh my God, did you see that?" she asked Em.

Em looked up distractedly from her book. "What?"

"The way Dex fist-bumped the water boy."

Em had missed it, Dex was being led off with the medic and the water boy in tow, and the ref was blowing his whistle for the game to recommence. There were six minutes left in the first half.

"Oh yeah," Em said drily, picking up her glass of wine from the coffee table near where her feet were propped. "How surprising for a jock to do that."

Harper laughed. Em's legendary affability with men did not extend to sports. She'd never been into it particularly, but having to constantly compete with the sports department for a slice of the funding pie at her school was an ongoing irritant.

If Em had her way, she'd have banned all forms of organised sport from existence. It was a testament to their friendship that she was watching the game at all. Sort of.

"Has he texted you yet?"

"No."

"Ugh." Em sighed. "*Men.* Why do they do that?"

Harper made what she hoped was a suitably vague noise indicating her own puzzlement, as she feigned interest in the game despite her give-a-shit wavering now that Dex was off the field.

"Oh my God." Em rolled her head to inspect Harper's face. "*You* contacted *him,* didn't you?"

Taking a sip of her own wine, Harper shrugged noncommittally, hoping in vain that Em might drop it.

"*Harper.*" Em might be the same age as Harper, but she had perfected that don't-mess-with-me schoolteacher voice very early in her career.

"Just a couple of texts." Harper could feel Em's stare lasering into the flesh of her profile.

She narrowed her eyes in suspicion. "And? What else?"

"Nothing," she lied, wishing Em would just send her to the naughty corner already and lose the stare of interrogation.

A very unladylike snort came from the woman who looked pretty and delicate and like she quite possibly farted rose petals. "You've had *sex* with him, haven't you? Since I saw you on Monday."

Harper dropped her gaze guiltily to the couch, thinking about the things she and Dex had done right where they were sitting. "Well…"

"Oh my God." Em jumped up. "*You had sex on this couch*, didn't you?"

"No." Harper shook her head violently. At least not in the time frame her friend was talking about, anyway. Best not go into that, though. Or the other time on the island bench where Em had sat earlier, drinking wine and prattling on about how stupid men were.

She'd tell Em later. When her man-hate had disappeared and they were back to sharing the intimate details of their lives like they had since they were six.

Harper grabbed Em's hand and yanked her back onto the couch. "It was only the once, okay? It was a…spontaneous kind of a thing."

Em kept hold of her hand. "So it was a…*booty call*?

Harper blinked. She hadn't thought about it like that. She'd never hooked up with a guy just for sex. Especially not one she didn't know that well. She grinned.

She'd had her first booty call.

"Well, yeah, I guess. *I* initiated it, though," she added hastily at the disapproving look on her friend's face.

"But…why?"

If Em hadn't been genuine, her puzzled expression would have been funny. Harper sighed. "Because he's just so easy to be with."

And that was the truth of it.

Of course, it helped that he was also pretty damn easy to look at.

"Oh no, *no,*" Em wailed. "Harper, listen to me." She squeezed Harper's hand tightly as she clasped it against her chest. So tight Harper almost winced. "This is the kind of thing *I* do. Not you. It's normally you holding my hand, telling me to slow it down, to not rush into things. And you were right. Booty calls mess with your head and make you feel shitty afterward, and you're my best friend. I don't want you to feel shitty."

Harper pressed her lips together so she wouldn't laugh. She didn't feel shitty. Hell, she felt sexy. Wanted.

Desired.

The difference between Em's booty calls, and Harper's one and only, was the type of guy and the expectations involved. Em attracted jerks and always expected a booty call to be a sign of something more.

The beginning of a commitment.

Not Harper. She had absolutely no expectations where Dex was concerned. They weren't a couple. They weren't even heading toward being a couple. What happened here on Wednesday afternoon was just two people who liked each other getting their rocks off.

Simple.

"It's fine, Em," she assured her bestie. "It's not like that between us. *Really.* I'm going to be fine."

Em didn't look convinced, dropping Harper's hand and pulling her in for a hard hug instead. "Just be careful, okay?" she insisted, her voice muffled in Harper's hair.

Harper rolled her eyes at the melodrama as Em's slender arms practically cracked ribs. "I promise," she assured her, wondering when old, resilient, unicorns-and-rainbows-Em was going to make a reappearance, because she wasn't sure her body was going to survive too many more hard squeezes from emotional-wreck-Em.

Harper opened her door at three sharp on Sunday afternoon. Behind her in the living room, Jace and Tabby were squabbling over whose turn it was to play the PlayStation, but their arguments faded to black as Harper took in the sight of Dex lounging casually in her doorway wearing shorts and a T-shirt, his hair damp.

He smelled fresh and clean and looked big and vital, a small laceration high on his forehead the only evidence of last night's bloody but temporary exit from the field. He brought both his hands from behind his back and held up two jumbo packs of chips.

"It's not a movie afternoon unless there are salt and vinegar chips."

Harper couldn't have agreed more. "This is true." She smiled, hoping she sounded a lot more nonchalant than she felt.

She couldn't believe how nervous she was. A big old knot in her gut was getting larger by the minute. She'd changed her outfit three times, finally deciding on a maxi dress that hugged her boobs, skimmed her curves, and had an Aztec pattern that was very flattering to her shape.

She'd fought the urge to apply makeup, settling for just a slick of lip gloss, a fact he'd obviously noticed, as his gaze zeroed in on her mouth.

It was because of the twins she told herself. She didn't want them to get the wrong idea about her relationship with Dex. Harper was perfectly fine with deceiving Chuckers, but not two eleven-year-olds with whom she shared some genetic material.

She and Dex were friends. Jace and Tabby didn't need to

know about the benefits part that had evolved between them.

He grinned, slid his hands onto her waist, the chip packets rustling as he dragged her against him. "Hey," he murmured against her mouth before kissing her long and slow, the deep rumble of his groan as intoxicating as the aroma of coconut that filled her senses and poured like a rum cocktail through her veins.

A loud thump came from the living room, and Harper dragged herself away with difficulty, shaking her head at him. "We can't," she whispered, a hand on his chest to hold him back from taking more. "The twins. I don't want them thinking there's something going on between us."

His lazy smile almost curled her toes. "But there is something going on between us."

Harper's breath hitched at his casual observation. "It's just sex," she said dismissively, as much for herself as for him and his toe-curling smile. "And that's not any of their business."

"Okay sure." He shrugged casually, but she was sure she could hear a slight edge to his voice. "If you want to lie to your siblings…"

"It's not lying," she said quickly. He was teasing, but it hit a nerve. "They're *eleven*. They're innocents. There are things they don't need to know."

"So who *do* they think I am?"

"A friend."

"With benefits?" He grinned.

Harper grinned back. "Not today, mister. Today is just pizza and a couple of movies."

"Okay, fine." He sighed with faux disappointment. "As long as you know that I'm going to spend every minute of it thinking about ways of getting you out of that dress."

Dex took advantage of Harper's temporary brain malfunction to give her ass a quick squeeze before entering the townhouse. She had to grip the door for a beat or two

before she was composed enough to face her little brother
and sister without blushing.

"Okay," Dex announced, a few paces ahead of her, the
chip packets behind his back, "which Star Wars is it today?"

Harper caught up to him and introduced the twins, who
seemed a little overawed by his presence.

Not that she blamed them.

It wasn't that they knew him—the twins took after her
and her arty side more than they did Chuckers and his sporty
interests—he was just a physically imposing kind of guy. And
then there was his undeniable aura. Charisma swirled and
crackled like a force field around him which was, apparently,
also detectable by children and not *just* horny twenty-three-
year-old women.

He produced the goodies from behind his back. "Who
likes chips?"

Jace and Tabby's eyes almost popped out of their heads.
Anthea was all about whole food and calorie counting—the
prospect of having a child with a weight problem was just too
much for her vanity—so treats were rare.

"Me, me, me," they chimed simultaneously.

And just like that, they fell under his spell, too.

Harper had to think hard to remember a time when she
enjoyed herself as much as she had today. The fact that Dex,
like Harper, knew most of the dialogue in the film line-for-
line won him major brownie points with the twins. And then
he went and won *all* the brownie points by ordering the pizzas
over the phone in a Darth Vader voice.

Harper doubted she'd laughed this hard in a long time.

They paused between movies to eat the pizzas. He asked
them about their school and what their hobbies were, and

Tabby was telling him about how she'd just started playing the saxophone when Jace interrupted with, "Are you Harper's boyfriend?"

Harper almost spat her mouthful of water all over the table then nearly choked trying to swallow it instead.

"Of course not," she said as soon as she could catch her breath. She shot a panicked look at Dex in case he thought they had heard the term from her. "I told you, we're just friends." She smiled almost maniacally at her little brother in an attempt to convey how *friendly* they both were.

"Like you and Em?" he asked.

A little hand clamped around Harper's heart. Jace, his face earnest, was so like their father sometimes. "Exactly like that," Harper nodded.

If she and Em were playing strip Battlefront and getting each other off at work.

"Isn't that right, Dex?" she said, nodding at him encouragingly.

Dex, a small smile on his lips, raised a sardonic eyebrow but joined in, saying, "Exactly."

Jace opened his mouth as if he was going to ask more questions, but Harper had absolutely no intention of answering any of them. "Who wants ice cream?" she asked, standing and making a big deal out of cleaning up the pizza boxes and paper towels she'd used as disposable plates. "I've got some rocky road in the freezer especially for you guys."

Actually, she bought it for Em's impromptu visits, because that's what besties did—enabled their friend's ice cream habit. She'd certainly not planned to feed it to her brother and sister tonight. Anthea would have a pink fit. But desperate times required desperate measures.

There were cries of, "Me, me, me," and Harper breathed a sigh of relief.

• • •

Less than ten minutes and four bowls loaded with ice cream later, they were all sitting on the couch watching the opening to *The Phantom Menace*. It wasn't Dex's favourite of the franchise, but it was fun watching it through the eyes of those who hadn't seen it before.

He glanced over the tops of the twins' heads at Harper. Even with the kids sprawled between them, he was aware of her and that bloody dress on a primal level. It swished when she walked and rustled when she moved, which was frickin' distracting as all hell.

He hadn't come over for that. *Seriously.* Her eleven-year-old siblings were here for crying out loud. He'd come because he plain old liked her. *And* enjoyed her company. Not to mention he liked kids, and Star Wars even more so. It had been a no-brainer for him.

But then she'd answered the door in that dress, with her shiny lips and her wavy hair all loose around her face and shoulders, and he remembered how into her he was, how much her curvy body turned him on. He remembered the feel of her ass in his hands and the way she moaned his name as she came.

And he'd been excruciatingly aware of her ever since.

Compartmentalising Harper and his desire for her was easy when they were apart. He was so programmed to put rugby first that pushing everything else aside was a matter of habit. But rugby, *apparently,* took a backseat inside her townhouse.

Today, every shift, every wriggle, every time she stood to get something, or laughed, or opened her mouth to speak to Jace or Tabby, his desire burned hot and bright and he wished like hell those two cute, funny kids were far the hell away.

Awareness of her prickled from his skull to the base of his

spine on a continuous loop.

He wanted her on her back. He wanted her naked. He wanted her legs twined around his waist.

Not touching her was torture, and every time he forgot and reached for her and had to stop himself, the pressure in his balls cranked up a little bit more.

Still, despite the sexual frustration, being here with her still beat the hell out of the usual way they celebrated a Saturday night victory, hitting the town on a Sunday night with Linc and some of the other single guys from the team. Which meant too much booze, and a parade of rugby bunnies after selfies and a quickie in a toilet stall if one of the guys was so inclined.

Sometimes even a strip club.

Dex shuddered. He hated strip clubs—and the lap dances that Linc loved so much and always tried to buy him. Skinny women in G-strings with pneumatic boobs gyrating around, eyes blank as they pretended it was the best job in the world.

That was normally the part of the night where he bailed and went home.

Mostly he just hated always being *on.* Being Dexter Blake, Sydney Smoke front-rower. Aware that people recognised him, and that made him a target. Fans were usually pretty good. They just wanted an autograph or to impart some friendly *advice,* but there was always someone who wanted to pick a fight.

And for damn sure someone somewhere *always* had a mobile phone, snapping off surreptitious pictures and video, uploading them without permission to social media and watching them go viral.

Linc loved that kind of shit, but Dex had never been into the sideshow that was fame. It was all such a trap, and he'd worked too hard to get where he was to be distracted by any of it.

Not to mention how fake it all was. With so many sycophants hanging around, how were young guys coming up through the ranks supposed to know who was genuine and who wasn't?

It was getting harder and harder for Dex to tell, and he'd been around for a while now.

Harper was genuine, though. He rolled his head to the side to watch her. She had her arm around Tabby, her hand absently stroking the top of her little sister's head.

Harper Nugent was the real deal. 100 percent diamond.

Nothing cubic about her.

And he'd known that from the beginning. From her reluctance to get involved with him in the first place, to her lack of artifice, to how easy it felt sitting here on her couch, Harper had been a breath of fresh air.

It felt good just being around her.

Being with a woman and not feeling any pressure was a revelation. Dex too often felt he was expected to act a certain way. To talk rugby all night, to throw a lot of cash around at a flashy restaurant, to be outrageously blokey.

But not with Harper. She didn't seem to have any expectations. She certainly hadn't asked for anything. She'd been happy to keep things low key and hang around with him *outside* the glitz and glamour of rugby. There was no pressure with her to perform, to be something he wasn't.

And that was way more seductive than a rugby bunny dropping to her knees in a toilet stall.

Chapter Nine

Jace and Tabby groaned and complained when the movie ended, stalling their little hearts out to stay a bit longer.

Dex shamelessly curried their favour by prolonging things with a batch of hot chocolate he'd whipped up on her stove, but eventually Harper called it a night.

"Come on, you two," she said, gathering their mugs and dumping them in the sink.

"Can't we stay the night?" Jace pleaded.

"No. It's school tomorrow," she said. "You know the rules. Now, *quick sticks*, I promised your mum you wouldn't be too late. Go get ready and I'll drive you home."

"I can take them, if you like," Dex said. "I'm going anyway, and they're on my way." He hadn't planned on leaving until much later, but if Harper had to drop her siblings home, it made much more sense for the guy who was leaving anyway to do it.

"Oh yes, *pleeeease*," Tabby said, sitting up in her chair and clapping her hands, then clasping them together as if in prayer as she looked at her sister.

"Please, Harper, please!"

Dex laughed as the twins pleaded in unison, with that strange twin thing they had going on. They may not be identical, but he'd noticed tonight how often they'd finished each other's sentences.

She blinked. Dex wasn't sure if it was to do with his offer or how quickly the kids had gone from begging to stay to pleading to go. "Oh…I don't know." She glanced at him, a tiny crease mark between her eyebrows. "I don't want to put you out. You don't have to do that."

Dex shrugged. "I know. But it's no bother."

"Pleeeease, we'll be *reeeeally* good," Tabby added for an extra dollop of emotional blackmail.

"Okay sure." She smiled at him, and Dex was grateful for the solid weight of the island bench at his hip holding him up as a big hand squeezed hard around his gut. "Thanks. I appreciate it."

He smiled back, locking his gaze with hers. "My pleasure."

Which wasn't entirely true. Being with her tonight had been the most agonising mix of pleasure *and* pain.

Her lips twitched, but she didn't look away from him as she said, "Okay, you two, you know the drill. PJs, slippers, and teeth. First one back here ready to go with all their stuff gets to sit in the front with Dex."

The twins took off like a pair of cartoon roadrunners. "I hope you don't mind," she apologised. "They respond best to a bit of healthy competition."

Dex couldn't have cared less. All he cared about was that they were alone for the first time in hours, and he wasn't going to waste an entire second. He strode across the kitchen in three paces, crowding Harper back against the sink and kissing her like it was his last hour on Earth.

He half expected her to protest, to push him away in case the twins came back and sprang them making out, but she moaned and clutched his arms, bunching the fabric of his sleeves, murmuring, "Yes, *God* yes," against his mouth as she kissed him back.

The roughness in her voice and the surge of his cock against the confines of his fly emboldened Dex, and he slid a hand to the back of her thigh, inching up the slippery material of her dress. He groaned when his palm finally hit bare skin and pushed under the fabric, heading north until he was squeezing a handful of her ass.

"God," he panted, "I've been wanting to get under this skirt all bloody afternoon."

And he kissed her again, sliding his thigh between her legs, pressing the thick wedge of it against the centre of her. She moaned and he pressed harder, the kiss suddenly exploding, careening out of control, their heads twisting and turning, their breathing laboured as each fought to keep up with the other.

Thankfully, a loud thump somewhere in the direction of the bathroom dragged them out of their sexual bubble, and they broke apart, his hand falling from her ass, his thigh unjamming itself from between her legs.

Dex shook his head to clear the thick fog of lust demanding he shove his thigh right back where it was and pick up where they left off.

"What was that?" Harper called out, her mouth still wet from their kiss.

"Just tripped over," Jace yelled.

She frowned but didn't have time to ask anything more as both the twins raced into the kitchen, Tabby just ahead of him.

"Yes!" she crowed. "I bags the front."

Jace looked like he was about to complain, but Dex got in ahead of him. "You can ride in the front next time, buddy."

Harper glanced at him, startled, her expression clearly

saying *Next time?* He grinned and shrugged. *Why not?*

"Say thank you and good-bye to your sister," he said, in his best Darth Vader voice.

Jace and Tabby laughed, but they enthusiastically hugged and kissed Harper. Dex was left in no doubt that not only did they love their big sister as much as she loved them, but they obviously thought she'd been at the head of the line when the awesome sauce was being dished out.

Dex couldn't have agreed more. Harper was awesome to the power of infinity.

At almost nine on Sunday night it was only a ten-minute drive to the twin's house, and it was a fun ride. Jace and Tabby kept giving him quotes to say in his Darth Vader voice, and they were all still laughing as the front door swung open.

A petite, immaculately coiffed woman in her early fifties opened the door. "Hey Mum," Jace and Tabby said in unison, hugging their mother in turn.

"Hello darlings," she said, eyeing Dex as she accepted hugs and noisy kisses. "And who's this?"

"Harper's boyfriend," Tabby said casually as she and Jace entered the house.

Dex blinked, as the older woman said, "Boyfriend?"

"She said he was just a friend," Jace added for clarification, "but we saw them kissing in the kitchen."

Dex blinked again. He thought about how far up Harper's skirt his hand had been buried and wondered just *how* much the two eleven-year-olds had seen.

"Boyfriend?" Anthea repeated, doubt colouring her voice, clearly having trouble wrapping her head around the concept.

His natural instinct to correct Tabby's preposterous

statement—*he didn't* do *girlfriends*—warred with the knowledge that the reason he and Harper were *seeing each other* in the first place was for her stepbrother and mother to think they *were* romantically involved.

He put his hand out. "Hi. I'm Dex. You must be Anthea."

"Dexter Blake?" The male voice drifted from somewhere behind Anthea, and Dex looked over her shoulder just as Chuck Nugent appeared. The twins had already called out their thanks and good-byes as they'd wandered into the house, so he was alone with Harper's two nemeses. "Hey, Chuck," he said, dredging up a polite smile.

"Nice to see you." Chuck stuck out his hand and pumped Dex's, his smile obsequious. "Come in and have beer," he said, standing aside.

"Oh, no thanks." Dex shook his head. "I have to be going."

Chuck took the rejection on the chin. "So…" he said enthusiastically, "you and Harper, huh?"

It was a good act but Dex was used to spotting fakes, and he could see the slight moue of distaste bending Chuck's mouth out of shape. Before Dex could reply, Anthea was lining up for a shot, too.

"Are you and Harper actually…*seeing* each other?" Unlike her son, Anthea didn't make any attempt to hide her incredulity.

Dex's ire stirred at the utter meanness of the question. He remembered the text from the restaurant, and the same anger he'd felt then boiled in his gut. If anything, it was worse, more acute now he'd witnessed Anthea's lack of compassion face-to-face.

"That's right," he nodded. "For a couple of weeks now."

"Oh." Anthea looked quite taken aback by the news. "I wouldn't have thought she was your…type."

Dex tightened his jaw, resentful that Harper was still being demeaned by people who were supposed to love her, and that *he'd* been stereotyped, as well. The urge to punch a hole in the nearby door rode him hard, and he stretched out his traps on one side of his neck then the other to dissipate the impulse.

After all, there was more than one way to call someone on their crap.

"Oh yes." He nodded. "She's *exactly* my type. I'm completely smitten. But please," he said, leaning in conspiratorially, encouraging both Chuck and Anthea to lean in, too. "Don't say anything to her, because I'm pretty sure she's just using me for sex."

A soft gasp escaped Anthea's mouth as the colour drained from her face. Had she been chewing on anything, Dex was pretty sure she'd be choking on it about now.

"Anyway," he said to the two stunned faces, "I'd best be getting on. Lovely to meet you, Anthea." About as lovely as a dose of food poisoning, and just as toxic. "See you around, Chuck."

Dex didn't linger for a good-bye, or even to see if they would recover from his deliberately provocative statement. He just strode away with only one thing on his mind.

He had to see Harper.

Twelve minutes later, Dex pulled up at her place and was knocking on her door. She was still in that dress, but she could have been wearing a sack as far as he was concerned. He just wanted to hold her.

"Dex?" She frowned at him, clearly not expecting him to have come back, although the slight tremor in her voice did betray her excitement that he had.

"I don't think I'm going to be invited to any Nugent family BBQ's in a hurry."

Harper laughed, folding her arms as she settled against the doorframe. "Oh no. What happened? Did you punch Chuck?"

Dex snorted. "No. But I may have…implied you were using me for sex."

She blinked. "*Implied*?"

"Well…stated is probably more accurate."

She laughed harder. "What the hell?"

"What can I say?" He shrugged. "They were pissing me off."

She fluttered a hand over her heart and gave an exaggerated sigh. "My hero."

His gaze fell to where her hand nestled against the roundness of her breast. *She was so soft there.* When Dex returned his attention to her face she was watching him closely.

"Thank you for defending my honour."

He chuckled. "By besmirching it?"

"Meh," she said dismissively. "Whatever works."

They grinned at each other for long moments. "Do you need to go home?" she asked.

Dex hesitated. He should. Griff had organised some ex-military guy who specialised in survival training to do some sessions with them. For some unknown reason these started at four in the morning—some crap about mental conditioning—and tomorrow was their first session.

"Not yet. What'd you have in mind?"

She pretended to ponder for a beat or two. "How about more Star Wars?" she mused, her face a picture of innocence.

"Not *quite* the stars I had in mind."

"Me neither." She grinned and grabbed him by the front of his shirt, pulling him inside.

• • •

Harper wasn't sure how—they certainly never discussed it—Sunday became *their* day. Over the course of the next month, spending the day with Dex and the twins became a regular thing. A couple of times they watched movies and ate pizzas. One time they played PG console games all afternoon, the guys versus the girls. Another time, Dex crammed a baseball hat on his head and donned dark sunglasses and they spent a few anonymous, fun-filled hours at Luna Park, riding the Wild Mouse roller coaster, eating too much fairy floss, and twirling around the Ferris wheel in the magnificent shadow of the Sydney Harbour Bridge.

In an attempt to flaunt their fake relationship—that's why they were doing it after all—Dex dropped the kids home to Anthea each Sunday night before turning around and driving straight back to Harper's, where the *adult* content of their day commenced. He never stayed the night, citing training as an excuse as he kissed her goodbye in the wee hours, but that was okay.

He always left Harper with a big smile and a satisfied body. What more could she want?

Em, still in her all-men-are-bastards funk, was the voice of doom. "Why are you letting him use you like this?" she griped, not assuaged even after meeting *and* being charmed by Dex one Sunday afternoon.

Harper, a bit weirded-out by their role reversal, just smiled and said, "We're using each other."

"He's told you he doesn't want a relationship. This is only ever going to be just sex for him."

"Fine by me," Harper smiled. "It's just sex for me, too."

"You haven't even been to his place."

Harper liked that *her* place had become *his* haven. She understood without him having to tell her that it was a place away from prying eyes for him. A place where he could just be himself. The fact she could give him that was immensely satisfying.

"He likes coming to mine."

Em would snort and leave it be for another a few days, but it was clear she thought Harper incapable of such casualness. She was wrong, though. Harper was embracing it whole-heartedly. Her previous relationships had been fraught with the expectation of progressing, of moving forward as a couple.

With Dex, she had no expectations.

Who the hell knew that could be so freeing?

• • •

The fifth week after their first Sunday movie day, he surprised her by inviting her to a home game instead. Occasionally they played on a Sunday or on a Friday night, depending on the comp schedule, and it was the Smoke's turn for a Sunday game.

"I know a way to really drive Chuck crazy," he'd said down the phone line.

To say Harper was stunned at his suggestion that she attend a game was an understatement. All she'd been able to reply with was an "Oh."

"You don't have to," he'd said. "Just thought it'd annoy the living crap out of Chuck to have you hanging out with the WAGS in the Sydney Smoke's corporate box."

Harper had smiled, acknowledging the truth of it. "I'd love to. Thank you."

She hadn't seen him play live. That first night they'd met she'd hadn't really known who any of the players were, so she hadn't paid him any particular heed. But she'd watched every one of his games on the television since and been impressed by his skill, his moves.

To see him play live would be awesome.

Annoying Chuck was a bonus.

"Good." She could hear the note of desire in his voice and felt a corresponding pleasure buzz through every cell of her body. "Come to the main entrance of the stadium at five. Someone named Eve will be waiting for you, and she'll take you through to the box. I won't be able to see you till after the game, though."

He'd hung up shortly after but the buzz lingered for a long, long time.

• • •

Eve turned out to be Griff King's PA, who greeted her with a friendly smile. She appeared to be about forty, and was in jeans and an oversize Smoke jersey, her hair scraped back with an ancient-looking scrunchie.

They chatted comfortably about the Sydney traffic and the impending game as Eve led Harper quickly and efficiently through the crowds to the corporate box.

And that was where Harper's comfort ended.

Half a dozen gorgeous creatures turned to greet her, their stares blatantly curious.

Fuck.

Harper's mind went blank as Eve performed the introductions, blindsided by how freaking *glamourous* the wives and girlfriends of the Sydney Smoke players were in real life. Like Eve, they, too, had teamed jerseys with jeans, but theirs were clearly designer labels, and they wore them with such confidence and sex appeal.

Harper always felt self-conscious in jeans—worried they were showing every lump and bump, every pocket of cellulite—but not these women. These women didn't look like they had an ounce of cellulite *anywhere*.

Christ. She'd made a huge mistake. She should have Googled these women. Then she would have been prepared.

Possibly even pulled out.

She felt gargantuan and, frankly, *fat,* amidst the svelte bodies that glowed with good health and expensive skin care. They could have been models. Come to think of it, one of them was…but which one? They could all have qualified.

How stupid was she just to rock up and not give any thought to how intimidating this might be. Why hadn't she been to the hairdresser? Gotten a manicure. *And* a pedicure. Hell, she should have gotten a freaking *Brazilian.* Why hadn't she worn one of her figure-flattering maxis instead of an ass-emphasising peasant skirt?

Why hadn't she worn her goddamn spanks?

"So lovely to meet you," said a petite woman, coming forward after the intros. A blonde pixie cut feathered around her face, complementing her overall slenderness.

Harper must have looked blank because the woman smiled and said, "Matilda Kent, I'm Tanner's girlfriend. Don't worry, I promise you we're all very nice. Here" — she reached down to a low table and plucked a glass of wine off a tray — "you look like you could do with a drink."

Harper clutched at the drink like a lifeline. Another woman named Valerie — a redhead with stunningly gorgeous freckles, who was actually the coach's daughter — approached with Eve, and they started asking Harper about herself and what she did, which drew the other women in. They bombarded her with questions, all obviously fascinated by her murals at the hospital, and Harper talked until the Smoke ran out onto the field and their attention shifted.

Harper was surprised to realise that these glamorous women were actually *nice* and that she'd relaxed.

"Liam's looking pumped tonight, Eve," Valerie said.

Harper followed Valerie's line of sight to see Griffin King standing with a companionable hand on the shoulder of the kid with Down Syndrome whom she'd seen on the television the other night. He was shuffling from foot to foot, obviously excited.

"When isn't he?" Eve laughed. "He takes his water boy responsibilities *very* seriously." She smiled indulgently as she glanced at Valerie. "Your dad's so good with him."

Valerie smiled at Eve, but it seemed a little strained to Harper.

"Liam's my son," Eve said, turning to Harper.

A groan came from a woman called Kathy who had her eyes glued to a mounted television set in one corner. "That's *Johnny,* you idiot."

Harper tensed at the sound of Chuck's voice as the camera panned around the field, and he put names to faces for the television audience. Kathy rolled her eyes at the screen. "God, he's *such* a dick."

In her peripheral vision, Harper could see Eve frantically shaking her head and making a cutting motion across her neck to Kathy. Kathy frowned, clearly puzzled by Eve's sign language.

Dex must have told Eve about Harper's relationship with Chuck.

"Don't worry, Eve," Harper assured. "There's no love lost between me and my stepbrother."

Kathy blanched. Somehow not even that ruined the beautiful planes of her face. "Oh God, he's your brother? I'm so sorry," she apologised, a hand pressed to her chest. "I didn't realise you were related."

"*Step*brother," Harper clarified, waving a dismissive hand. "Don't worry about it. Chuck *is* a dick."

There was general laughter, then the ref blew his whistle and everyone's attention was focused on the game. By the time halftime rocked around, the guys were in front, the mood in the box was buoyant, and Harper felt like one of the gang.

Or at least she didn't feel like a giant interrupting a dolly's tea party anymore.

These women may be impressively beautiful, but they were also just wives and girlfriends wanting their men to do well. They were friendly, involving her in their chatter, which surprisingly didn't revolve around the guys or rugby. Instead, they talked about their families, and problems at work, and the latest movies they'd seen or books they'd read.

Toward the end of halftime, they were talking about a black-tie event, a fundraiser for the City Central kids hospital in a month's time, which all the guys had been ordered to attend. Harper knew the event. She'd been asked to go by the hospital executives, as they were planning to showcase her work in a special effects presentation, lighting up the venue walls with some of the murals she'd already completed.

She had been flattered and accepted. But before she could add to the conversation, the guys were running back out, ready for the second half, and all attention returned to the field. Harper was sipping on her third wine as the ref blew his whistle for start of play.

"So, you and Dex, huh?"

Harper startled at Matilda's low question to her left. "Oh no," she assured. Harper didn't want it to get back to Dex that she'd implied *anything* about their relationship. And she wanted to be upfront with Matilda and all the other WAGS that she wouldn't be joining their ranks.

There was no way she belonged amongst this elegant assortment of women, no matter how welcome they'd made her, or how awesome it felt being here.

"It's nothing, really. We're not a…*thing*. We're just friends."

Matilda quirked an eyebrow. "With benefits?"

Harper lowered her eyes from the shrewd probe of Matilda's gaze, deliberately finding Dex on the field and locking on him. "It's nothing serious," she evaded.

"Oh, I don't know," Matilda mused. "Dex has never invited a woman into the box before, according to Tanner."

Harper refused to let the implied significance take hold in her psyche. Other people were bound to make assumptions at seeing them together. Which was the appeal of staying away from anyone who *could* make assumptions.

Nobody speculated about their *relationship* when they were shut away inside her house.

"We're really just doing it to annoy Chuck," she said dismissively, keeping her eyes on Dex. And not just to discourage conversation—mostly because she found it hard to drag them away.

Matilda seemed to take the hint, which was a relief, leaving Harper to her outright ogling of Dex. Conversation ebbed and flowed around her, and she participated where required, but otherwise she let her gaze follow him around the field, zeroing in on the incredible hunk of bone, muscle, and sinew that made up his body. The corded strength of his arms as he reached up and plucked a ball from the air. The power of his quads as he ran down the field. The tight bunch of his glutes.

All muscles he happened to use to devastating effect between the sheets, too.

Harper glanced around her. Every woman here was equally focused on the field, sitting forward in their seats, hands clenched, nostrils flaring as they clocked their own guys.

Were their thoughts as dirty as Harper's?

Were they as *aroused* as she was?

Chapter Ten

The Smoke won by eight, and Dex was high on their victory two hours later as they climbed out of the car. He'd laughed and joked throughout the trip to her place, swirling patterns up her leg with his index finger as he drove, recounting some of the night's best plays, leaning over to kiss her senseless at every red traffic light.

Harper knew exactly how he felt, already charged-up from watching him strut his stuff on the field. But then there was the added stimulus of the way he smelled, the aroma of soap on his skin and coconut in his hair. Add in the testosterone pouring off him, and there was one hell of a heady mix going on in the confines of the car.

He was damn lucky she hadn't jumped him at one of those traffic lights. As it was, the door to her place had barely shut before Harper was on him. Yanking his shirt off. Kissing him hard and deep. Fumbling with the tie of his shorts. Yanking his wallet free as they slid down his legs.

"Slow down," he groaned as he tried to kick out of his shoes and his shorts all while being moved inexorably backward by Harper in full heat.

"No," she murmured as his legs hit the couch and she pushed him down onto it. He winced as the slight graze on his shoulder blade from a stray boot came into contact with the arm, but Harper didn't care.

He looked like an underwear model stretched out on her couch, the type that adorned billboards. His right leg lay along the length of the couch but his left thigh was spread wide, his knee bent, his foot flat on the floor, exposing the big, beautiful bulge stretching out the front of his Calvin's.

That bulge and all the acres of man flesh surrounding it were all she cared about.

She needed to be *on* him. To have all that hard, solid body under her. To harness for her own satisfaction that surge of power she'd witnessed on the field.

All she'd been able to think about as she'd watched him was his absolute dominance during the game. He played like nothing could tear him down.

Watching him duck and weave and bust through walls of muscle like a great marauding beast had been a huge turn-on. Because she knew *she* could bring him to his knees with one shake of her ass.

And it had totally brought out the Neanderthal in her.

Her pulse pounded like jungle drums through her head. She shoved the foil packet she'd liberated from his wallet between her teeth as she reached behind her for the button and zip of her skirt, cursing her shaking fingers.

"Take your shirt off," he panted as he watched her struggle through slitted eyelids, making a grab for the hem.

Frustrated, she abandoned the idea of taking her skirt off, whisking her shirt off over her head instead, then rucking her skirt up and quickly stripping off her underwear

"And the bra."

Harper shook her head. "Later." She couldn't coordinate

skirt, knickers, condom, *and* bra.

And right now, condom took precedence.

She straddled him, one knee on the couch next to his right thigh, the other pressed hard against the outside of his left, just north of his bent knee. She gripped his body tight between her legs as her fingers ripped open the foil.

He groaned when she yanked his underwear down, barely acknowledging the beauty of his erect cock in her hurry to sheath him. Then she was grabbing for his big naked shoulders, dragging herself up higher, lining up their hips.

"Harper, wait," he panted as she reached for his cock. "My head's spinning."

"Good," she rasped. She didn't want to wait. She wanted to *fuck*.

Her hand closed around him as she lifted herself over him, guiding him to her entrance. She didn't pause or tease, just sank herself down with a strangled gasp, her fingers digging into the balls of his shoulders, her head falling back as he slid all the way home.

"*Fuuuck*," he groaned, his hands clamping hard onto her hips, his eyes squeezing shut.

Harper couldn't move for a beat or two. She could barely breathe as she adjusted to the depth of his high, hard possession. But then she couldn't *not* move. It was as natural as her heartbeat, as waves falling on sand, as night becoming day.

Primal forces took over, her pelvis rocking to a beat that couldn't be heard but wouldn't be denied, either.

"Harper," Dex whispered, his eyes opening as she started to undulate her internal muscles up and the down the length of him. His hands reached for her breasts, her nipples tight and hard against the fabric of her bra as he cupped them, squeezed them.

"*God*. You're so sexy," he said, his gaze roaming over her

face and the hair tumbling in what felt like complete disarray around her shoulders. "You look like a gypsy."

And she felt like one, too. Wild and free. A complete wanton who knew what she wanted and how to get it.

And right now it was Dex.

She flexed her pelvis, and they both moaned at the movement. Then she did it again. And again. Lifting on and off little by little, more and more each time, until she was withdrawing almost completely on the upstroke only to take him all the way in again as she slammed down.

She rode him with complete abandon, leaning into her extended arms, her hands anchored to his shoulders and the counter force of his big, palms flattening her breasts.

She grunted her appreciation with each entry, the rigid girth of him almost slicing her in half, jolting through her like an electric shock, hurting *so damn good*.

She didn't want to stop.

She didn't *ever* want to stop.

But she needed completion, too, so she rode him faster, vaguely aware of their pants and gasps, of his thighs trembling beneath her, of a ball of light tightening and contracting deep in her belly like a constricting pupil. It blew out in one almighty burst, pushing her above them both, tossing her about and turning her around, battering her with rain and light and pleasure until she couldn't physically take anymore, and then it whirled her back to Earth.

"Christ," he said, as she collapsed, gasping, against his chest, his cock still rigid and unfulfilled inside her. "That was fast."

Harper gave a half laugh, her lips at his neck. "What can I say? Watching you play rugby makes me horny."

His fingers lightly stroked her back. "In that case, I'll get you a season pass."

She sighed as he continued the drugging caress, shutting

her eyes enjoying his lazy touch. "I'm sorry," she murmured, rousing after a minute. Her breathing had begun to return to normal and awareness was starting to creep back in, particularly of his cock still buried hard and deep inside her. She propped herself up on her elbow. "I shamelessly used your body to get off and was too impatient to wait for you."

"Just so you know, you are welcome to shamelessly use my body to get off any time you want."

Harper laughed. "You're so easy."

"I prefer to think of it as accommodating."

She deliberately squeezed her internal muscles, clamping hard around him. He sucked air in through his teeth. "You're going to pay for that."

His abs tensed then he was suddenly sitting, taking her up with him. "Hold on, baby." He slid his hands under her ass before rising to his feet. Harper gave a little squeal as she held tight. "I'm going to make you come so hard you're going to want to name a day of the week after me."

And with that he strode into her bedroom as if she weighed no more than a football.

Hours later they lay in her bed, exhausted and quiet, a faint red glow coming from her bedside lamp over which she'd thrown a fringed red chiffon scarf. It would have been quite romantic had Harper's belly not rumbled loud enough to wake the neighbours. She laughed, slipping her hand over it. "Sorry. It's feeling neglected."

He rolled up onto his elbow, smiling as he slid his hand over top of hers. "Well, I have been very demanding of you. But if you're hungry, I can make a mean mac and cheese."

She laughed. The idea seemed absurd at this hour. "*You* can make mac and cheese?"

"Oh yes." His smile faded a little as he propped his chin on her chest. "As long as it comes from a packet. And you have a microwave."

Harper shuddered. "Mmm. Delicious. *Not.*"

One side of his mouth quirked up. "Hey, if you add real cheese, it's practically gourmet."

"*Yummy.*"

He rubbed his chin absently against her chest. His whiskers prickled, spreading goose bumps down her body, beading her nipples. "It keeps you alive," he said after a beat or two. "And it's cheap."

The sensation fanned up her neck, too. Or maybe that was more to do with his sudden seriousness. Something told her this was a subject with which he was very familiar. They hadn't really talked about his background, other than him hinting that his path to professional rugby hadn't been clear sailing.

She sifted her fingers through his hair. "Sounds like that's something you know about?"

"A misspent youth," he said, trying for a smile that didn't quite reach his eyes.

"Oh? Where was that?"

For a moment she thought he was going to change the subject but then he relented. "Perry Hill," he said.

Perry Hill? That was a public housing estate of the worst kind in Sydney's west. High crime, low employment. Truancy, poverty, despair.

It was real wrong-side-of-the-tracks territory.

"You've come a long way," she said tentatively. "Is your family still there?"

He shook his head, his whiskers rubbing. "No. They moved north. The warmer weather is better for my dad's health. They have a nice house by the beach now."

Harper didn't have to ask to know that he'd been

responsible for that. "No more mac and cheese, huh?"

He grimaced. "Not if I can help it."

"Your dad's not…well?"

He shifted, flopping onto his back. Harper rolled up this time, propping her chin on *his* chest. His arm came up around her, his hand resting on her shoulder.

"He had a work accident when I was a toddler," Dex said, staring at the ceiling. "He has some paralysis. For the most part, he needs a wheelchair to get around. Work didn't pay out, said it was his fault. They made a couple of poor financial decisions trying to fix things, which only put them more into debt. He was in and out of hospital. Expensive operations. They lost the house. They had three little kids. He couldn't find work, and when he did his hospital visits made him unreliable. There was nothing put away for a rainy day. Nothing for his retirement. My mum worked two jobs just to keep that shitty Perry Hill roof over our heads and my dad in operations and pain meds. There wasn't a lot of money for fancy food."

Harper watched his mouth as he spoke. His lips, set in a grim line, barely moved. He'd done it tough. Having lost both her parents, Harper knew tough. But this was a different kind. And both sucked.

She understood now why he was so determined to put his career before all else, what he was fighting for. The boy from Perry Hill was future-proofing himself. "I'm sorry," she whispered, running her finger down his nose, over his lips and down his chin.

He shook his head as if he was coming out of a trance. "Hey." He smiled, looking at her again. "At least I can cook, right?"

She smiled back. "A man who can cook is a marvellous thing."

She kissed him then, ever-so-lightly, before pulling away and snuggling her head onto his shoulder, trying to give him comfort just from the press of her body.

Absently, her hand wandered—it was hard to stop with so much temptation at her fingertips. She stroked down his body, traced patterns on his hips, over his flat abdomen, and up his chest to his pecs.

He was flat in places, ridged in others, but deliciously smooth, the only hair the dark whiskery goodness of his neck. Even his legs were shaved, as was the trend for athletes these days.

He reminded her of a canvas. Blank yet full of possibilities.

Their conversation faded as desire took hold. And she knew just the thing to distract him from the past.

"You don't have any tattoos," she mused absently. Most of the players on the field tonight, from both teams, seemed to sport at least one or two on their arms or legs or both.

"No."

"A lot of the other guys did."

"You were checking out the other guys?"

Harper smiled at the note of fake gruffness in his voice completely ruined by the hint of amusement. "Only to check they were okay as they lay scattered on the ground in pieces after you busted right through them."

He chuckled. "Good answer."

"You don't like them?" she asked as she swirled her index finger around his nipple. "Tattoos?"

"No. I don't mind them. I just prefer to take my pain on the footy field."

Harper smiled, an idea forming rapidly in her brain. She sat, kissing him briefly. "Wait here." She scrambled to the side of the bed. "I'll be right back."

"I really should go," he called after her.

Harper glanced over her shoulder, satisfied to note his gaze was glued to her ass. Her bedside clock said ten past one. It was usually about this time he was kissing her good-bye, but she was gripped with the urgent desire to keep him in her bed for just a little bit longer. He'd opened up to her tonight, and she wanted to give something of herself, too.

"Just another half an hour, I promise." She grinned before slipping out the door.

She was back within a few minutes, several small paintpots in a handy wire basket carrier, along with a few dainty paintbrushes, and a drop sheet tucked under her arm. Her breath caught as she stared at his naked, sleeping form. Even relaxed his muscles were magnificently defined, their bulk hinting at the power leashed by slumber.

Her gaze drifted to the elegant length of his cock. It might be flaccid now, but its size and girth hinted at all its glorious capabilities.

She had the sudden urge to paint him like this—relaxed, his body a study of actual and potential energy.

But...another time.

She had something different in mind tonight.

"Get up, sleepy head," she said. His eyes fluttered open as she threw the clean but paint-flecked bundle on the bed at his feet. "I need to put this drop sheet down."

Dex lifted his head, eyeing it. "It's not plastic is it?"

"Don't worry." She grinned. "You're the only Dexter here tonight. No chainsaws, I promise. Just these." She held up a handful of small artist's paintbrushes. "I'm going to ink you. It'll be *awesome.*"

He laughed, but moved. Between the two of them they covered her bed with the sheet, and within seconds he was lying in the centre while she straddled his knees, the basket with the paintpots sitting on the mattress nearby.

Harper knew exactly what she wanted to create as she dipped her brush into the black paint. "Christ that's cold," he said as she made her first stroke mid-thigh, his balls visibly contracting. "What are you painting?"

"It's a surprise," she murmured, using broad brushstrokes to bring her vision to life.

He ground his knee against the juncture of her thighs, and Harper sucked in a breath, her eyelids fluttering shut. "God," he muttered. "You're still wet."

She shifted away from the wicked press of his kneecap, forcing her eyes open. "Behave," she said, "or I'll paint dicks all over you."

He laughed. "You expect me to just lay here and do nothing while you lean over me all naked like that?"

She shot him her best prim look. "Yes, I do. The more you mess about, the longer it will take. You want to see the end result or not?"

"Fine," he sighed, lifting his arms above him, bending his elbows and tucking his hands under his head as he glued his gaze to the ceiling. "I'm all yours."

A tiny trill fluttered through Harper's stomach. It felt like he'd been all hers for the past month.

What would it be like to have *that* forever?

She worked quickly, aware of the hour yet still absorbed in her work. His hairless thighs were the perfect canvas for the dark red and ochre flames snaking upward. His cock hardened as the flames licked his groin and his lower abdomen.

She glanced at him, quirking an eyebrow. "Seriously?"

"You're naked and that damn paintbrush feels like your tongue," he bitched. But desire crackled in his gaze, as wicked as the flames climbing his legs. Her own desire ignited, heating until it sizzled through her blood.

"Tell me what you're painting," he said, raising his head to look down his body.

"Patience," she murmured.

Harper reached for a finer brush once she got to his abdomen, swirling it over his flesh in lighter strokes, curling plumes of smoke in gray and black over the ridges of his belly, the indent of his ribs and the flat planes of his pecs. The smoke crossed over at his nipples before dispersing into vapour over the broad round planes of his shoulders and the base of his throat.

She was conscious of his eyes on her as she worked, conscious of each infinitesimal reaction of his body to the light stroke of the brush—the quickening of his breath, the slight twitch of muscle, the fine shiver as cold paint kissed warm flesh.

By the time she was done, her breath clogged her throat, thick as fog.

"Watching you paint is turning me on," Dex murmured as she sat back to admire her handiwork.

Harper smiled. "Now you know how I feel." She threw her paintbrush down, satisfied. "Done," she said. He lifted his head to look down his body. She pointed to the door of her wardrobe and said, "Go look in the mirror."

She lay on her side in the middle of the bed, her elbow bent, her head propped on her flattened palm, and she held her breath as he opened the door and inspected himself in the full-length mirror, twisting and turning to see all the detail. The low light in the room was a perfect complement to the art, casting the red of the flame in sharp relief while shadowing the darker, airier wisps of smoke, giving them a sense of motion.

Had there been time she'd have done his back, too, with more flames bubbling like dragon scales across the broad expanse.

"You're right." He looked at her with eyes full of wonder and admiration. "This is *awesome.*"

Harper let out her breath, thrilled at his obvious delight. "It helps to have a decent canvas."

He nodded slowly as he headed toward her, potently sexy with his thighs aflame, his gaze fixed firmly on her breasts. "I couldn't agree more."

Harper swallowed as he neared, the arousal she'd felt as she'd brushed paint over his body flushing bright and hot through her system, settling like a nest of prickles between her legs.

"My turn."

Harper barely heard him over the beating of her heart in her ears. "From memory, you're not great with paint."

He crawled onto the bed and she rolled onto her back as he straddled her hips, the broad canvas of his smoke and flame chest dominating her view. Her breath hitched at the pure raw power of him.

"I'll keep it simple," he said as he reached for a paintbrush.

Harper shivered as he traced the round fullness of her left breast with cold black paint. He used the brush in the red paint next to repeat the process. He followed it with another circle of black. Then red. Then black. Each circle grew smaller and smaller until he was skimming her areola and her nipple was an achingly hard point.

She waited for the cold paint to touch her nipple, her insides melting in anticipation, her hands screwed tight in the drop sheet. But it never came. Instead, he paused to admire his handiwork.

Harper clenched and unclenched her hands as she looked down at herself. "Are you painting a bullseye?" she asked, incredulous.

He grinned. "I might be."

Harper laughed and shook her head, but endured as he repeated the process on her right breast, the nipple begging for attention and again left wanting.

"Now what?" she asked huskily.

"The pièce de résistance," he murmured, choosing the thicker brush that Harper had used for the flames. Dipping it in the black, he painted a long line from her sternum down to her pubic bone. He dipped again, thickening the line until it was about an inch wide, then painted a triangle at the southernmost point.

"Well?" he asked. "What do you think?"

Harper looked at the thick black arrow pointing the way straight between her legs. She smiled momentarily before clearing her throat for a professional critique. Kind of hard when she was painted with two bull's-eyes and an arrow, her nipples shamelessly betraying her state of arousal.

"It's kind of abstract…but not terrible."

"Oh baby." He grinned. "There ain't *anything* abstract about it. *That's* a promise."

Harper's blood flowed thick and hot through her pelvis, flooding the ache between her legs. She should tell him to go. That he had to be up for training at six. But she wanted him to follow through on that promise so freaking bad.

And he did, shuffling back quickly, pushing her legs apart with the broad intrusion of his shoulders, settling himself between her legs and fixing his mouth to her.

"I take it back," she gasped, her back arching as his tongue got busy and his hands found their bull's-eyes. "You're *really* freaking good with paint."

He didn't answer. She would have killed him if he had.

• • •

Dex stirred slightly, lightening a little from the heavy layers of sleep some time later. Harper shifted, her body seeking his. Sexual satisfaction weighted him to the bed, and he revelled in it, letting it pull him under a little deeper as her head burrowed into his shoulder and she settled her thigh over the top of his.

"I love you," she murmured, her lips nuzzling his chest, her breathing slow and deep.

Somewhere in the quagmire of slumber, his chest flooded with pleasure at the knowledge, and his eyes fluttered partially open. For some reason he couldn't fathom, it was stupidly light in the room. The scarf must have slid off the lamp.

He shut his eyes again, drifting along in that strange twilight zone between consciousness and unconsciousness with Harper warm and soft at his side. He'd never met a woman like her—someone who gave so openly and didn't want anything in return.

Who he could be *himself* around.

Someone who understood him. Who hadn't judged him over his roots like so many people in his past had done. Who liked *him*, not just the trappings of his celebrity. Who had no expectations.

He'd told *her* she was awesome a dozen times, but actually *this* was awesome. This...*thing* between them. Them together. Rugby had been everything to him for so long, but now there was something else.

Harper Nugent ticked all his boxes. *And* she loved him.

Something buzzed loud and insistent nearby, bringing him slowly out of slumber again. It took long seconds to register the noise as his phone, but the message finally got through, piercing the bubble and dragging him by the roots of his hair into full consciousness.

He sat bolt upright, the bright morning light stabbing into his eyeballs as he displaced Harper. "Fuck," he said, his heart racing like a train on a track as his phone jangled through his nerves. He grappled to orientate himself, looking around wildly for the phone or the time, or any sense he could grab hold of.

"What time is it?" he demanded. He'd zeroed in on his phone, discarded on the floor, and groped for it.

"What?" she asked, blinking at him sleepily, her smudged bull's-eyes and black arrow a startling reminder of last night's fun and games and the fact that he was at Harper's.

He'd stayed the night at Harper's.

And she *loved* him?

Jesus.

He reached his phone and snatched it up. It was Tanner. "Where the fuck are you?" he demanded, ignoring any preliminaries. "Griff is *pissed off*. Wherever you are, you better be dead because he's probably going to kill you if you're not."

Griff had been one of the best rugby players the world had ever seen. Now he was the best damn rugby coach alive. And Dex knew how lucky he was to be coached by the best. Sure, Griff was a tough taskmaster. He demanded 100 percent from everyone, but he gave 200 percent in return.

Never miss a training session was one of his golden rules.

Jesus. With his brain coming back online he could see the clock on Harper's bedside table announcing the time as a quarter to seven. Training started forty-five minutes ago.

Dex had *never* missed a training session. He sure as hell had never been late for a one. He'd seen Griff bench guys for a hell of a lot less.

"I'm coming now," he said, springing out of bed wondering where the fuck his clothes were.

He caught his reflection in the mirror as he paced around the bed. Christ, he was still covered in paint, dried and cracking, and no time to shower.

"Your clothes are near the couch."

Harper's voice was calm and clear as she jogged his memory, which was more than could be said for him as he went into full-blown panic mode. He couldn't afford this kind of slip up. He might not have lived on the wrong side of the tracks for over a decade, but the lessons from that time in his life were as fresh as yesterday.

This shit was how you got busted from the team. How things went to hell. And a kid from Perry Hill was never arrogant enough to think it couldn't happen to him.

Holy crap! His chest was tight and his fingers had started to tingle. He didn't bother to thank or acknowledge her help, just turned for the door and strode out.

He found his clothes and threw them on, his heart pounding as he sat on the couch to tie his shoes, his brain tossing around potential excuses *and* various routes he could take to get to the stadium as quickly as he could now that Monday morning traffic would be in full bitch.

Christ. What the fuck was the matter with him? *This* was why he didn't get involved with anyone. *This* was what being involved did to a man's concentration. He more than anyone had had to fight for his place on the team, but bring out a bloody paintbrush and he lost his mind.

"Are you okay?"

Dex stiffened. "*No.*" He yanked the lace on his shoe.

"I'm sure Griff'll—"

He yanked the other one and stood to face her. She was in a T-shirt that stopped high on her thighs, and if he was a betting man he'd place money on her being naked underneath. His body responded to her in a completely Pavlovian way that ratcheted up his anger another notch, disgusted at his lack of control.

"You sure Griff will what?" he demanded. "You don't know the first bloody thing about Griffin King and what he will and won't do."

She raised both her eyebrows and put her hands up in a *whoa there* motion. "Okay. Sorry, you're right."

Great. Now he was yelling and taking it out on Harper because *he* was torn. *Jesus.* He'd never been torn before. He'd always known where his priorities lay.

And he hated that she'd muddied the water for him. Hated her. Hated himself.

"So what *will* he do?" she asked.

"At the very least, he'll bench me for the next game. At worse, he'll castrate me with his bare hands."

She gave a hesitant half laugh. "That's a bit dramatic, isn't it?"

Any hold he'd had on his temper snapped with a twang that practically rattled his teeth. "I'm late for my goddamn training session. Griff doesn't accept *late*." He shoved a hand through his hair. She wouldn't understand. How could she? She grew up playing video games while he ate packet mac and cheese.

He hadn't just let his focus slide—he'd let *Griff* down.

The thought made him half crazy.

"*This* is why I said I didn't do dating and relationships. *This* was why we were just…hanging out and having fun. But then *you*"—he glared at her, wanting to shake her so she would understand—"go and say the *L* word and now I'm late for practise."

She recoiled as if he had struck her. "What the hell are you talking about? I did *not* say the *L* word."

"You did. Before. In your sleep. You said 'I love you.'"

God was it only a handful of minutes ago that the sleepy words she'd uttered had sounded so damn good in his slumberous drowse.

What had he been thinking? It was a fucking *disaster*.

Harper looked stunned at the revelation, her olive complexion draining to white. She seemed temporarily speechless before she straightened her spine.

"Take a freaking breath, Dex. I once apparently told my father in the middle of a very sound sleep that I was in Narnia. I'm pretty sure he didn't take it as gospel."

Dex had waited for her denial. Yearned for it. But now it was here, it didn't bring him the relief he'd hoped for. It only made him want to grab her and shake her even more.

For fuck's sake. Where the hell was his head at? "This is

the kind of distraction I just don't need."

"Well, go," she said, her back stiff, her arms folded. "I'm not bloody stopping you."

Dex grabbed his keys from off the floor where they'd fallen a handful of hours ago and strode to the door. He paused when he got there. "I can't do this anymore."

She frowned. "Do what?"

"This," he said, turning to face her. "*Us*. Obviously it's more distracting than I realised."

Her look could have refrozen melted polar ice. "What on Earth makes you think I *ever* want to see you again? Don't let the door hit you in the ass on your way out."

Then she turned on her heel and stormed out of the room.

Chapter Eleven

"Something more important you had to do?" Griff inquired, his voice low and icy, as Dex ran onto the field forty-five minutes later.

The Smoke's coach was a big lion of a man. Only in his early forties, his hair was liberally shot with gray and a permanent frown crinkled his face into harsh lines. Apparently women found that sexy instead of terrifying. There was an insanely popular Facebook fan page devoted to him, complete with his own memes.

Obviously they'd never been at the wrong end of his ire.

There were times when Griff could yell loud enough to let everyone in the surrounding suburbs know his displeasure. But it was his quiet, menacing fury that was the most dangerous.

Fuck.

"No, boss. I…" Nothing short of an apocalypse or admission to intensive care was going to satisfy Griff.

"It's complicated," Dex said grimly. "But it won't happen again."

His eyes glittered a tawny yellow. "You've taken care of it?"

Dex nodded. "I have."

"Good." He pointed to the field behind him. "Lucky you, you get to drill twice. And you're benched for Saturday's game."

Dex used his fury at himself and Griff's punishment to get him through the gruelling session. They were always physically challenging, but having to do everything twice pushed him to his limits. By the time he'd hit the locker room he'd never been so exhausted in his life. Only a few hours sleep, combined with an exercise programme specifically designed by Griff to make grown men cry after just *one* run through, had left him utterly spent.

No such thing as gentle recovery swims as far as Griff was concerned.

The guys were mercifully devoid of smack talk—for the moment, anyway—obviously pitying him as he sat his sorry ass on the low bench. Also, Linc had the floor, talking about some chick he'd met at a club last night, and Dex had never been so thankful for Linc's big mouth and bigger ego.

Perspiration poured off Dex and every muscle quivered in a gelatinous soup as he leaned forward on his elbows and cradled his head in his hands. Aromas of sweat and grass and muscle liniment surrounded him.

"You okay?" Tanner asked, his voice low as he sat down beside Dex, his legs on the opposite side of the bench.

"I've been better."

"You need to talk about anything?"

Dex shook his head. Tanner was his skipper and his friend, but they didn't talk about their personal shit. And that was just the way Dex liked it.

"You know…" Tanner hesitated. "Griff is a goddamn genius. At *rugby*. But he's got nothing outside of it, Dex. His personal life is a wasteland. Don't try and emulate a guy who's so emotionally stunted he can't even bear to look at his own daughter most of the time."

Dex shrugged. "He's been through a lot."

Griffin King never talked about the tragedy that had poleaxed his life twenty years ago. Neither did anybody else, not even between themselves. It was taboo. "And he's alone," Tanner added. "Alone sucks."

"Fuck me," Dex said, trying to lighten the mood. "Tilly really does have you by the balls, doesn't she?"

Tanner grinned. "She's the best thing that ever happened to me."

Dex blinked at the statement. "What?" he half laughed. "Better than *rugby?*" If Dex has been asked to put money on it he would have said Tanner's priorities were to the game first.

"I'd give it up tomorrow if she asked me to."

Dex waited for Tanner to grow a second head or do *something* to indicate his apparent demonic possession.

"Look man," said Tanner, "I think you really like this chick. I haven't seen you serious about anyone, and I've known you since under nineteens. Don't fuck it up."

Maybe Tanner was right. Maybe there was more to him and Harper hanging out. Maybe there was more to the fucking than just friendly benefits. But he couldn't think about that now. He wouldn't *let* himself go there.

"I'll worry about all that shit after my career is done."

Tanner groaned. "Don't make her your consolation prize, man. Jesus, don't you know anything about women?"

"Only what Linc tells me," he said with a humourless smile, tipping his chin at Linc, still flapping his gums.

"Christ, that's a worry." Tanner grinned. "What Linc *thinks* he knows would take up all the space on the frickin' internet. What he *really* knows could fit on the back of a postage stamp."

Dex laughed. Linc talked a lot of shit, but at least he was focused on the game first and foremost, too.

"She won't be around, man," Tanner continued. "Some other guy will have snapped her up, and you'll be too damn old and broken-down to beat him up."

The thought of Harper with someone else hammered inside his head, filling Dex with the unreasonable urge to smash his fist into the nearest locker. Although Tanner's face might be a good alternative if he didn't *shut the fuck up*.

He dropped his head from side to side to stretch out his traps, then stood in case he succumbed to the impulse. He needed a shower. He needed to be alone. He needed to crawl into his bed and die for a couple of hours.

He needed to forget about Harper Nugent.

Signalling their *conversation* was over, he stripped his shirt off as he strode the two paces to his locker.

A wolf whistle rang out around the room, echoing off the tinny lockers and he realised too late about the paint on his body.

Fuck. There went his moratorium on smack talk.

"Don't look now Dex," Bodie said, "but I think you're on fire."

"Smmmmokin'," Linc called in his best Jim Carey voice.

"Cool ink, man," Donovan added. "But you should really ask for your money back. It's a little smudged."

A lot of Harper's swirling smoke was either smudged from rolling around on the sheets with her, or had run in streaks from the sweat that had dripped down his body. But it was largely still recognisable.

"So, that's where you were," John Trimble mused. "I hope it came with a happy ending."

Dex grabbed a towel from his locker and slammed it shut. "Why don't you ask your mother, Johnny," he snapped, and strode away.

Laughter followed him all the way to the shower.

• • •

It took two weeks for Dex to crack. His life had gone to hell in a handbasket, and he hated it. After being benched for that one game, he'd been raring and ready to go for the next one, but he'd screwed up, including fucking up a line out that had led to the other team scoring a crucial try and winning the match.

Griff had been apoplectic, but no one had taken it harder than Dex.

His training was suffering, too. Once upon a time, rugby had filled his head from morning to night, especially during those sessions on the field when he was pounding away and sweating like a pig, giving everything he had and more for the game and for Griff. Now, all he could think about was Harper.

The things he'd said to her that last morning. The *L* word on her lips.

How much he missed her.

And he got no relief from his thoughts at night. In the dark, when his mind finally let up enough to drift off to sleep, his dreams turned steamy and he'd wake with a start, his body aching, reaching for her, desperate for her touch.

Christ, if there were a worldwide award for wanking, Dex would win it with flying colours. He lay in the dark night after night, his hand on his cock, conjuring her face, her smell, the feel of her hair brushing his stomach, only to be left with a limp dick and that sick, hollow feeling in the aftermath.

Because no amount of instant gratification could make up for her absence.

He felt the loss of her acutely every moment of the day. It weighed heavily on him even during training, ruining his concentration. And every time he fudged a tackle or dropped a ball, Griff grew grimmer and grimmer.

Dex got so desperate he let Linc take him to a strip club, thinking he might find some distraction there. A woman with hips and thighs. Someone with whom he could close his eyes and pretend he was with her. But none of the women did a damn thing for him, and he was left to his own devices yet again.

He didn't know what kind of wild female juju Harper had going on, but she had crept under his skin and he was hooked.

When the fuck it had happened, he had no idea. But he did know he needed to fix it.

Pronto.

He needed her back in his life. He needed things the way they were. Then maybe his world could return to its regularly scheduled programming.

Rugby six days a week, and Harper on Sundays.

• • •

He wasn't nervous when he knocked on her door. His heart was pumping for sure, but that was from anticipation. Even if she kicked him out he'd get to see her again, and frankly, he'd give his right nut just for a glimpse.

He'd waited till six, figuring she'd be home from the hospital and any sibling wrangling she had to do by now. If she wasn't home, he'd wait for her. He'd done it before, and he'd been nowhere near as desperate as he was now.

He should have rung. Or, at the very least, texted. It would have been the polite thing to do. But he didn't want her to hang up on him, or give her a heads-up he was coming over.

He wanted her at as much of a disadvantage as he was where she was concerned.

The door swung abruptly open, and he couldn't say who

was more taken aback—Harper, from the unexpected sight of him after two weeks of radio silence, or him, at finding her in her long red dressing gown with Japanese symbols stitched in yellow cotton down the front panels. Her hair was piled on top of her head, and there was a towel slung over her arm.

He'd bet his other nut she was naked beneath.

Neither of them said or did anything for a moment. But he could hear the roughness of her breath, echoing his own, and see the wild dilation of her pupils. "Go away," she said finally, crankily, slamming the door in his face.

But he was too quick, catching it before it shut, holding it open against the insistent push of her arm. "Please," he said, "I just want to talk. I have something to say."

"I don't want to hear it," she said, her voice glacial.

"I'm not leaving until I say what I came to say."

She glared at him, obviously weighing up her chances of winning a tug-of-war with the door and concluding she wouldn't win.

"Fine." Her hand dropped from the doorframe. "But I'm going out, and I've got fifteen minutes to have a shower, get ready, and be out the door, so you better talk fast."

She pivoted away, stalking across the lounge area and heading for her bedroom. Dex had no choice but to follow if he wanted to talk to her. "Where are you going?" he asked as he stepped into her bedroom in time to catch the swish of red fabric entering her en suite.

And with who?

He followed her into the bathroom. She was throwing the towel up over the glass of the shower screen when he caught up. Dex halted at the line where the wooden floorboards of her bedroom met the tiles of her bathroom, leaning against the doorjamb. It seemed like it was a line he probably shouldn't cross anymore, although, God knew, that seemed to be their thing.

"To a movie," she said, looking over her shoulder at him, "Not that it's any of your goddamn business."

"Are you going with someone?"

She quirked an eyebrow that perfectly conveyed just the right amount of you-have-to-be-shitting-me. "Yes."

Dex decided to quit now. If she told him it was a guy, he didn't trust himself not to do something drastic like drag her up against him and kiss her until they both couldn't breathe.

He shoved his hands in his pockets just to be on the safe side. He was supposed to be winning her back, not demonstrating how much of a caveman he could be.

"I came to apologise for that morning."

"Oh really?"

Dex couldn't tell what *oh really* meant. Her voice was neutral, so was her face. She wasn't giving anything away.

"Yes. Really." He tried to inject every single ounce of his remorse into the two words.

She stared at him for long minutes. "Okay, fine. Thanks," she said flippantly. "Don't let the door hit you in the ass on your way out."

She pulled the shower door open, but Dex moved quicker, his hand landing on her shoulder to stop her from getting in. If nothing else, he needed her to know he *was* sorry. "Please, let me explain."

The angle of her jaw tightened as her gaze flicked to the hand on her shoulder. Dex could feel the stiffness of her frame through the palm of his hand.

"Fine," she said, her fingers quickly untying the belt of the robe and wriggling her shoulders. His hand fell away, so did the gown, slithering to the ground and pooling at her feet. "You have ten minutes."

The breath hissed out of his lungs as acres of her flesh were exposed to his view. "*Holy fuck…*"

Was she being deliberately provocative or just practical?

She was supposedly in a hurry, and it wasn't like he hadn't seen her naked before.

Dex would have liked to have done the gentlemanly thing and averted his gaze but it was just not in his power. In fact, he flat out ogled her—the thrust of her breasts and the tight points of her nipples, olive skin, soft belly, rounded hips, legs that were long and strong.

His Xena, warrior princess.

"Nine and a half," she said, her lips twisting in a bitter smile as she stepped in and shut the door after her.

The glass of the shower stall had a wide band of frosting half way up, obscuring everything from mid-thigh to her shoulders.

In other words, the *good* bits.

And it didn't seem to matter how hard he stared at it, the glass remained stubbornly frosted. Running water added background music to the amateur porn film that was currently running through his head.

Him opening the door and stepping in. Her telling him she was a dirty girl. Him picking up the soap and offering to *cleanse* her.

Christ.

It had a predictable effect inside his jeans, and Dex wished he'd worn a less *snug* pair.

"Nine!"

Fuck. Little less ogling and a lot more conversation, idiot.

Dex took a deep breath to steady the crashing of his heart inside his ribs. "I'm sorry about walking out like I did. I was in full panic mode. I wasn't…thinking straight."

"I've never asked you to stay the night, Dex. In fact, I've never demanded *anything* of you, and I sure as hell didn't have you tied to my bed."

"I know," he said quickly, wishing she'd used a little less sexual imagery but grateful she was at least talking now. Her back was to him and he watched as water sluiced over her nape and the top two notches of her spine. "I was shocked and angry at *myself* more than anything. I guess I'm always a little paranoid that it's all going to end and I'm going to be back on the bones of my ass in Perry Hill, which is why I've *never* been late to training. But that was my fault, and I took it out on you. Which was wrong of me, and I'm sorry."

"And yet it took you two weeks to figure it out."

"No." He shook his head. "I pretty much knew I'd been a dick straight away. But I figured…a clean break was best. Better you hated me anyway, right?" He gave a grim smile she couldn't see because her back was still turned and she was busy lathering herself up with soap.

Of course. Fuck. *Kill me now.*

He took a pace toward the mirror then turned and settled his ass against the vanity, staring straight ahead at the open doorway instead of the soap bubbles sliding down her neck.

"It just took me two weeks to realise I *can't* keep away. Nothing's the same, Harper. My concentration is shot, my focus is blurred, and my football has gone down the crapper."

"Ah. So this is about *rugby.*"

Dex's hands tightened into fists as he mentally rejected her bald statement. Yes, he wanted his on-field mojo back, but it was about *more* than rugby.

And if he hadn't known that before he came, he knew it now.

"It's about not being able to get you out of my head. About how much I like having you in my life. How much I like *being* with you. How much everything *works* better with you around."

"Jesus, Dex, you make me sound like a maid. Or a can of bloody WD-40."

"I'm sorry. I'm not very good at this kind of thing. And—" He stopped himself before he said what he was about to say.

"And?"

"It doesn't matter," he dismissed. He was trying to win her favour not piss her off with his ill-conceived, testosterone-driven thoughts.

"For God's sake, Dex, *you're* the one who barged in to here to explain yourself, so just say it, will you?"

He sighed. "And thoughts of you all wet and slippery are not helping my articulation."

She didn't say anything for long moments. "So it's about sex, too?"

"No," he denied, despite his raging hard-on. It *wasn't* just about sex, either.

"No?" Her voice sounded incredulous. "Not even if I were to tell you I'm touching myself right now?"

The air in Dex's lungs shunted to an abrupt halt as he glanced at her, startled. Her back was still to him, water still running down her neck where a few wet strands of her updo had come undone. One palm was pressed flat against the tiles above her head. The other... He was damned if he knew where the other one was, or what it was doing.

"Harper." He hadn't meant it to come out so growly, but his control, which had been pretty slender since she'd answered the door in her gown and then shrugged out of it right in front of him, stretched a little thinner.

"Haven't you thought about me like this, Dex?" she asked, her voice husky.

Dex stood slowly, turning to face the shower recess. His balls had pulled unbearably tight. "*Harper.*"

"Do you know women can have wet dreams, too?" she asked, a slight pant to her voice as she ignored the raspy warning in his.

He shut his eyes, paralysed both by the question and an image of her, her breasts pressed against the cold tiles, her hand buried between her legs.

"I didn't know that till these last couple of weeks, but I've actually woken up drenched and almost coming sometimes, confused about what's happening but then I remember what you were doing to me in my dreams. *God*, Dex, *those dreams…*"

Dex swallowed. He couldn't see her touching herself, but her fingers curling into the tile above her head, the knuckles whitening, the hitch in her breath, were filling in the blanks.

"Yeah," he said hoarsely, suddenly finding it difficult to breathe. "I've been having them, too."

"Well?" she demanded, her voice low but plenty pissed off. "Are you going to get in the goddamn shower or do you want a written invitation?"

Dex blinked at the unexpected command. What the fuck? She *wanted* him to join her?

"*Dex!*"

He guessed that was a yes.

He should tell her no. Should insist they talk. Should stay the hell out of the shower. But he *couldn't*. Not even if his life had depended on it.

Responding to the desperation turning her voice to gravel, he stripped out of his clothes in ten seconds flat, quickly sheathing himself with a condom. His hands shook as he opened the glass door and stepped in.

"Dex," she panted, looking over her shoulder at him, her gaze dropping to the jutting evidence of his arousal. She arced her back slightly, thrusting her ass in his direction. "*God…*I'm so damn close."

Her feet were evenly spaced apart, separating her legs, and although he couldn't see where her lower hand was exactly, her bent elbow was obviously not idle. Water hit her nape and ran over her ribs and spine, sluicing over her ass and down the backs of her thighs.

She looked glorious. He wanted to sink to his knees, grab

her ass cheeks and bury his face in the heat and wet between her legs.

"*Dex.*"

The raw need in her voice spurred him to action. He didn't stop to ask her what she wanted—his body knew on a primal level exactly what that was. He slid in behind her in one easy stride, one hand gliding up her belly to claim a breast, the nipple like a bead in the centre of his palm, the other gliding between her legs, displacing her own.

"Yes," she gasped, pressing back into him, the length of his cock jammed between her buttocks. Her hand slid up high on the tiles, joining the other, the knuckles also turning white as Dex zeroed in on the hard knot of nerves between her legs and rubbed.

He tried to kiss her but she turned her face, his lips landing on her cheek instead. He should have been annoyed or insulted. He should have been worried it was a bad sign, but all he could think about was getting inside her.

His heart thundered against his rib cage, as did the corresponding pound of hers, their bodies perfectly aligned as he guided the head of his cock to the slickness between her legs. Her thighs were trembling, and she moaned at each hard stroke over her clitoris, but still managed to angle herself just right, eager to accommodate him.

Dex grabbed hold of an ass cheek and slid inside. He groaned out loud, but it wasn't enough to drown out Harper who came *hard* when he entered her. His pulse roared at her complete loss of control, and he thrust, quick and relentless, prolonging her pleasure, building his own rapidly, no thought of holding back or delaying his own release as her desperate, mewing cries catapulted him out of his body and he came lightning fast, burning bright and brilliant, his essence streaming out with a hot, pulsing force for long cataclysmic moments before finally fading away, leaving a delicious simmer humming in his blood.

Hands still high on the walls, Harper sagged against the tiles. Dex followed as he slowly came back to himself, the fronts of his thighs bracketing the backs of hers. He nuzzled her temple as their breathing returned to normal, the drum of the water on the tile floor loud in the silence.

Eventually he moved, easing out of her body as his hands slid to her waist, and he wrapped his arms around her, kissing up and down the slant that joined neck to shoulder.

Dex wanted to stay like this forever.

She had other ideas.

"I thought you said you couldn't do this anymore?" she said finally.

He shrugged. "I can't not do it, either."

There was more silence for a while, then she squirmed against him and said, "I have to go."

His arm tightened around his waist. "Harper."

"I really need to get ready," she said. "Just go, okay?"

He tried to turn her around but she clung to the tiles, refusing to budge. "Harper don't you think we need to talk about us…about this?"

"Damn it, Dex." She turned her head and glared at him, amber flashing in the depths of her eyes. "I said go."

Dex blinked at the vehemence in her voice and the set of her chin. *What the fuck had just happened?* She'd practically ordered him into the shower, where they'd rutted like a pair of animals, not even *kissing,* and now she was kicking him out?

What was going on with her?

But the set to her chin had gotten more noticeable, and he knew now was not the time for psychoanalysis. Now was the time for retreat and reevaluation. To give her some space. To give them *both* space to wrap their heads around wild-animal shower sex.

With the greatest of difficulty, Dex dropped his arms and turned away. He stepped out of the shower, grabbed a towel off the rack and scooped his clothes up off the floor.

He didn't look back as he strode out of her bathroom. He didn't *go* back. He didn't think about who she was meeting. He just towelled off, threw on his clothes, and left.

But it damn near killed him.

Chapter Twelve

Harper crawled into bed in her robe after she got out of the shower. She couldn't go out now.

Not after…

Em, who had conveniently forgotten how many times she'd curled up in bed and cried for days after her succession of breakups, hadn't been impressed with Harper cancelling.

"Trust me on this. Staying at home and wallowing is a bad way of getting over a breakup."

There was nothing worse than a reformed doormat.

"It really is just a headache," Harper had pleaded. "Besides, you can't break up with someone you weren't really together with in the first place, can you?"

But even as she'd said it, Harper had known she was talking crap. Because the truth was, however they'd classified their relationship, she *had* fallen in love with Dexter Blake.

Was in love with Dexter Blake.

She just hadn't realised it consciously—obviously her subconscious was more clued in than she was—until he'd walked out two weeks ago with a full head of steam.

But she was 100 percent, whole-enchilada, full-catastrophe, in love with the guy. And not just because he was a hottie of the first order. Harper groaned and stuffed her hands between her legs thinking about what that hottie had just done to her in the shower.

Her attraction to him went much deeper. He'd been kind and sweet and gentle with her. His rescuing her like that at the rugby match, even when she hadn't needed it, still took her breath away. He'd championed her against Chuck and Anthea and been a massive boost to her ego.

The fact he could never seem to get enough of her, of the bits of her she'd always hated and lamented, had made her see herself in a different light. But it wasn't just about her boobs and her ass. He'd been interested in her life. In *things* and… stuff. Like her parents and her childhood, the intricacies of her job, and her hopes for the future.

He'd even wheedled out her plans to open a gallery one day, and she hadn't even fully articulated that to herself yet.

And, good lord almighty, he was good with the twins. Funny and jokey with them both. Kind and complimentary to Tabby, and a little bit blokey with Jace, sensing, as Harper could, his desperation for a good male role model. Chuck, for all his faults, was good with his brother, too, but he wasn't around much, and Jace really responded to Dex's innate ability to tease and praise in equal measure. Both of the twins adored him.

Any guy in her life had to pass muster with her brother and sister, and frankly too many of them had failed.

Simply put, he was all that and a bag of chips, and had completely stolen her heart. He'd had her from *Dex the Stud*.

And it sucked.

Because she was pretty sure he didn't love her back.

She was *damn sure* he liked *being* with her, liked her company, in and out of bed. But that wasn't the same thing.

Did she really want to hang around waiting for the end of his rugby career, waiting for him to have *time* for her?

A hot well of grief rose in her chest, sitting there like a bloody great boulder. She'd been in love a couple of times before—for two sparkly weeks at the age of fourteen, and at art college for a few fun months when she'd been nineteen—but not like this.

They seemed petty and juvenile, practise runs in comparison to this...*thing* sitting on her chest, weighing her down, making it impossible to breathe.

Harper castigated herself for her weakness with him earlier. Having sex with him in the shower hadn't helped matters. Sure, she hadn't planned on dropping her gown. She had *really* just wanted him to say his piece and go, but the second they'd stood in her tiny en suite together, her body had *craved* and so had his. She'd seen it in his eyes.

And a part of her had wanted to exploit the hell out of that weakness.

But she'd set them on an inevitable path, and when her soapy hands had headed south, brushing her inner thighs, she hadn't been able to stop herself. She'd wanted him there with a white-hot heat, and nothing else had mattered. Not the fact that he didn't love her, or the fact he loved a *ball* more. Her desire and arousal had been too great, her battered heart—*her pride*—no match for her roaring need.

But it hadn't taken long afterward for shame to set in.

I can't not do it, either. A few weeks ago, she had revelled in having that kind of sway over his body. But that was then. When they were just hanging out and having fun. When it was physical only. Or so she'd thought, anyway.

But now her heart was in it. *And his wasn't.*

His body was committed, and she assumed she could avail herself of that whenever she damn well pleased, but how long before she wanted *more?*

How long before she *asked* for more?

And what would happen then?

Harper sure as hell didn't want to find out. Their whole prior relationship seemed to have been predicated on her *not* asking anything of him.

It was best to keep things severed between them—wild-animal shower sex notwithstanding. He'd made it clear where his focus lay and *why*. She only had herself to blame if she blindly ignored that and expected him to change.

Powerful demons rooted deep in childhood were always hard to shake. She had to let him go. Move on. Be strong.

Starting with not losing her head, *or her clothes*, should he knock on her door again.

• • •

Unfortunately, Harper found out she just wasn't that strong. Not where the man she loved was concerned.

She opened the door to him the next night, and he'd barely said two words to her before she was dragging him inside and he was going down on her on the couch. It seemed kind of moot to protest when he came by the next night and the next. Not when she'd already invited him into her house and body twice, and her craving for him was growing.

In fact, the sex was so damn good, it completely hijacked Harper's determination to keep things severed. It was hard to be strong when his kisses were so bloody tempting.

Had his lips been dusted in cocaine, they couldn't have been more addictive.

By their third time, she was thinking that maybe what they had *would* do. Maybe having the bit of him that was left over after rugby was *better* than having it all. Especially when he gave it to her so unreservedly.

It sure as shit was better than having *nothing*.

She got the fun and the sexy times and not the hard stuff. The mundane and boring stuff like laundry and bills and taking out the garbage. And with him leaving in the middle of the night, she didn't have to worry about him farting in his sleep, or about morning breath.

Those things that quickly bogged relationships down.

She got to exist with him in a bubble kept afloat by this heady, sexual thrill, the prospect of a relationship that never staled or cooled off. Where the desire always burned bright. Where there was a permanent state of horniness.

And her love was big enough for both of them.

But that all came crashing down the following week as they lay in bed in the afterglow, lazily touching in the soft red light blanketing the room. Harper tried not to read too much into how often he was coming over. Prior to their breakup, they'd been a Sunday-only thing. But he'd been over five nights out of seven.

Did that mean something?

"Are you going to this fundraiser thingy on Friday night? For the City Central kid's hospital?" she asked.

"Mmm," he said.

Harper's lips curved. She didn't have to look at him to know his eyes would be closed. She knew that sleepy *mmm*. He sounded like that just before he fell asleep, his voice low and rumbly as he drifted in a semi-conscious state.

She rolled onto her side and he shifted, lifting his arm to accommodate her as she snuggled her head in the crook of his shoulder and closed her eyes. She shivered as his fingers trailed sensuously up and down her arms.

"I'm going as well," she murmured. "Why don't you swing by here, and we can go together."

His fingers stopped abruptly, and her eyes opened, aware of the sudden firming of his pectoral beneath her cheek. "You're going?"

His voice was sharper, less rumbly, and Harper could tell he was wide-awake now. She blinked into the warm red glow around her as a wave of goose bumps crawled up her nape. "Yes. They're doing a segment on my murals."

"Oh." His whole body seemed to grow tense beneath her. Had he not been toasty warm he could have given marble a run for its money. "You never said."

Well, no…she hadn't said. But she hadn't been deliberately withholding it from him, either. They just didn't really…talk about things. They kissed and fucked and slept, then he left and they started all over again. When they did talk, it was about the mural she was working on or the last game he'd played or the game he was about to play. Sometimes the twins.

Then they kissed and fucked and slept…

"It slipped my mind."

Silence enveloped them. And not the drowsy, postcoital, heavy with bone-deep satisfaction one of a minute ago. No. This was chock full of tension. She could almost hear his brain cranking over.

Harper frowned, not sure what his problem was. He may not want to hear the *L* word, or commit to a forever kind of relationship with her, but they were still *hanging out*, right? And they *had* been out in public together before.

"But as we are both going," she said, her voice as light and quivery as her confidence, "I thought it might be nice to go together."

He shifted his arm out from underneath her, displacing her as he sat and swung his legs out of the bed. "I wasn't going to go with anybody," he said as he reached for his discarded shirt and threw it on over his head.

Harper stared at his back as he slid his legs into his snug boxer briefs. A cold fist squeezed around her heart. "Are you worried I might make inappropriate jokes about rucking?"

He stood as he pulled the underwear up, and she caught

a brief glimpse of taut ass before it was encased in snug black cotton. He turned to look at her, his eyes roaming over her with his usual thoroughness. "I'm just not ready to go… public with us yet."

"Okay…" What the fuck did that mean? It wasn't like whatever the hell they were doing was a secret. "But we've been out to a wine and paint restaurant *and* to Luna Park. You asked me out in front of a handful of your teammates at a rugby game. Hell, I've been in the Smoke's corporate box at Henley stadium."

"Yes, but…*everyone* will be there." His eyes drifted to her breasts before returning to her face. "Sponsors, the media, the WAGS…"

He looked at her helplessly, and the hand squeezed a little harder.

Was he…worried how it would look rocking up to a glamorous event with someone who wasn't a size six on his arm? Was he trying to tell her that she couldn't possibly play in the same sandbox as the glamorous creatures she'd spent a fun few hours with at that home game?

Christ. Did he think she didn't *know* that?

The thought cut hard—harder than any insult her stepbrother or mother had handed out over the years—and she reached for the sheet, pulling it up her body, tucking it in under her arms as all the old feelings of inadequacy crashed in.

"And I'm not quite the image they have of a rugby union star's girlfriend, right?" Her heart beat with a sick, heavy heat, like molten rock in her chest.

He looked at her blankly. "What?"

Harper sucked in a breath, trying to stem the hurt haemorrhaging in her chest. "You're e*mbarrassed* to be seen with me," she stated, proud of how calm she sounded when she was dying inside.

It sure as hell explained why he was so keen to always stay in. Harper had loved that he'd felt at home in her home, but she'd thought that was about privacy, not secrecy.

When all along he'd been *ashamed* to take her anywhere.

They'd joked in the beginning about her being his dirty little secret, but it looked like she actually *was*.

"Don't be ridiculous," he growled, dismissing the statement with an impatient wave of his hand. "You should know by now that I can't get enough of you. Why on earth would you think that?"

Was he joking? Was he seriously kidding her now?

"Maybe because I have no *fucking* clue what the hell we're doing here, or how you *feel* about me."

"God, Harper, please," he said, shoving an exasperated hand through his hair. "You know I think you're awesome."

Awesome?

Harper snorted. Loud. It was that or burst into tears. "Awesome?" Hot tears scalded the backs of her eyes, but she blinked them back. "What are you, like, five?"

She thrust back the sheet and scooped up her discarded gown from the floor, sliding into it as she stood.

"You didn't seem to mind the compliment a few weeks ago."

He was right. She'd been happy when he'd told her she was awesome. But she'd moved on. And awesome was wholly fucking *inadequate*.

She was *in love* with him for fuck's sake. Awesome was an insult.

She tied the belt of the gown tight. "And just *why* am I so gosh-darned awesome?" she demanded, tossing her hair over her shoulder, glaring at him. "Because I'm no serious threat to your career? Because I don't make any demands? Because I'm a pushover? You knock on the door and I open my *goddamn* legs for you?"

"No!" Dex shook his head vehemently.

But Harper was on a roll, the hard ball of hurt inside her morphing into simmering rage. "Because I don't expect anything from you, don't pressure you for anything? Because you've got the best of both worlds—a steady supply of sex with absolutely no commitment. And I'm just good old Harper who's been stupid enough to go along with it. Well, guess what, Dex, I'm not going to be your dirty little secret anymore."

He took a step toward her. "It's not like that."

"Oh really?" She quirked an eyebrow. "Okay, then. Take me to the gala on Friday night."

He hesitated. It was barely perceptible, barely ruffled the air, and yet it hit her in the centre of the chest like a punch. Harper steeled herself to stand upright despite the winding force. She *would not* crumple in front of him.

He shook his head. "No. But please let me explain—"

"*No?*" Harper swallowed at the second blow, trying to tamp down a tide of rising hysteria.

This was her fault. All her fault.

What the hell had she been thinking tacitly agreeing to this half-life with him? She deserved this punch in the gut right now because she'd let him take her for granted.

"Harper…" His earnest green gaze begged her to understand. "I just need more time to wrap my head around all this. I just want to enjoy what we have for the moment."

She snorted. "I bet you do."

"No, I mean…I don't want to *share* you with anybody. I want to keep it private and personal while we can. You have no idea how crazy the speculation gets with the media, and *God,* if the WAGS get wind of anything between the two of us they'll never leave me alone. It's a distraction I don't need."

And there was the third blow. Nothing and *nobody* could be a distraction from his precious career. She understood the demons that drove him, and the last thing Harper wanted was to stand between him and rugby. But why in hell couldn't he have *both?*

Plenty did.

Dex may have talked himself into thinking he could drop out from the human race. Become some rugby bot with tunnel vision. But…*you don't always get what you want.*

And if he wanted her—if this truly wasn't about her being more Xena than Tinkerbell—then it was going to be on *her* terms.

"Well, that's too bad, Dex. Because I love you and I want the whole messy, distracting enchilada. I want a *relationship* with all the expectations and pressure that brings. I'm not going to be happy to just sit by and let it all be about you and your career. Not anymore. If you want me, then you have to be in all the way, Dex. This is a two-way street and I'm not settling for some half existence in your shadow. I don't care how good the sex is."

He shoved his hands on his hips. "You love me?" His face blanched, his complexion looking washed out in the eerie red glow of her bedside lamp. "You told me that was just something you said in your sleep."

"I lied," she snapped.

"Christ." He snatched up his jeans off the floor and yanked them on. "*Why* do you want it all?" he demanded, more incredulous than angry, the bed between them about as wide as the Grand freaking Canyon. "You think it's easy being the partner of someone who plays team sport at an elite level? Because it's *bloody hard.* Riding all the ups and downs with them. Early mornings and club demands, worrying about injury and sickness, and whether I'm picked for a world cup team, and dealing with me when I'm not. Then there's money and salary caps and contract negotiations, and the pressure to retire, and travelling a lot of the year, and the bloody vultures in the media who'll skew anything at the merest whiff of a scandal. Is that what you want your life to be?" he yelled across the bed at her.

Harper almost cried at the question. *Of course she fucking did.* "*Yes*," she yelled back. "That's what happens when you decide to be with someone. You're there for each other. Halving the burden. You know, for better for worse."

He looked at her startled, his eyes going all big and crazy as Harper realised what she said. "Oh, take a breath, Dex. I'm not about to start humming the wedding march at you. I just want to *be* with you."

"You *are* with me," he insisted.

"Yeah. *I* am." She shook her head. "But *you're* not with me."

It was no use. She could tell how freaked out he was with just one glance. She'd never met anyone who could compartmentalise his life so succinctly. And no matter how much she loved him, she wasn't going to settle for less. The way Dex had loved her body had taught her she didn't need to take any man's scraps.

She was damned if she was going to take his.

She lowered herself to the bed, her back to him. "I think it's time you left," she said, overwhelmed by the hopelessness of it all. She needed to be alone, to give into the crushing grief in her heart and the hot, insistent prick of tears.

She sat for a beat or two, holding her breath, conscious of him standing behind her, willing him to go, yearning for him to stay. The pressure in her chest and behind her eyes built and built until she didn't think she could stand it any longer.

"I'm sorry," he said.

And then he was gone. She heard the front door open and shut and it was only then she let the first tear fall.

• • •

Em, who had somehow miraculously deciphered Harper's distressed phone call, made it over in twelve minutes. Normally, it took her a good fifteen to twenty, but it *was* one o'clock in the morning.

"I'm sorry," Harper said, eyes streaming and nose running as her bestie appeared in the doorway. She'd never been so grateful to see those wild caramel curls in her life, even if she did look like a rumpled angel next to Harper's dishevelled hag.

But when didn't Em look gorgeous? *She* should be a WAG. Harper hiccupped at the thought, more tears threatening.

"A white or something stronger?" Em asked, producing a bottle of wine and a bottle of her old faithful—butterscotch schnapps—from behind her back.

White wine was usually Harper's drink of choice, but tonight she finally understood Em's attraction to something stronger when matters of the heart were concerned. "Schnapps."

There was nothing like a friend with an apartment key who came to you at one in the morning, no questions asked, and brought good booze. Yes, Harper had done it countless time for Em, but the reciprocation was still appreciated.

Em left the bedroom and Harper could hear her clinking around, obviously grabbing shot glasses. She was back in under a minute, kicking off her shoes and climbing into the bed. She handed Harper the shot glasses and filled them almost to the top.

They tapped them together and threw it back. "Dear God," Harper rasped as it clawed at her throat and ripped out every hair from her nostrils to her nether regions. She may never need to pay for a Brazilian ever again.

"I told you." Em grinned. "Exactly what you need to forget a guy."

"Forget a guy?" Harper blinked, trying to clear the

splotches in front of her eyes. "I think I've forgotten my *own* bloody name."

"Another?"

"Fuck yes," she said, holding up her glass.

They sipped this time, settling back against the headboard, Harper resting her head on Em's shoulder.

"Tell me what happened."

Harper blurted it all out in a tumble of tears and sniffling and schnapps. Em had known that Harper and Dex had parted ways and that Harper was in love with him, but not that Harper had started sleeping with him again. She felt mildly guilty about not telling her—they did, after all, tell each other everything—but Em waved Harper's blubbered apologies aside.

"So you've been having sex with the ex," Em said, cutting to the heart of it when Harper had finally run out of words. And tears.

Harper shook her head, depressed at the question. "How can I have? He can't be an ex if we were never a thing in the first place."

Em seemed to consider that as she poured a third schnapps for them. "So you two have just been a series of booty calls for him?"

Harper's face crumpled at the thought. Apparently there *were* more tears to be had.

Yeah, that's what she'd been. Willingly, too. Being Dex's booty call had been exciting in the beginning. Now she couldn't believe she'd demanded so little from him.

From herself.

"I've been his dirty little secret," she said, miserably.

"Oh, baby." Em put her arm around Harper's shoulder and kissed the top of her head. "So, what are we going to do about it?"

Harper looked at her friend warily—she'd heard that

note before. "No voodoo dolls. Or re-virginising."

"Spoil sport." Em laughed. "No. I have a better idea. You wear that sexy red dress you bought and have never worn to the fundraising gala, and you flirt and dance with every guy there."

Harper pulled away, settling herself farther back against the headboard. "Oh no." The last thing she wanted was to go and mingle with the glamorous people. Dex might have denied her curvy figure was the reason for his reluctance to go public, but her confidence had taken an almighty wallop. "I'm not going."

"What?" Em blinked. "You *have* to. Your murals are being featured. You're giving a speech about them."

Harper shook her head. She couldn't stand the thought of having what she couldn't be a part of rubbed in her face. "They can still showcase the murals. They don't need me to speak."

Em tsked. "You know your problem, don't you?"

"Yeah. Three dress sizes."

"You don't think you're worthy," Em said, ignoring Harper's belligerent reply. "Deep down, you've been okay with this dating in your house thing because you're still buying into the stepdouche's taunts and don't think you're worthy of being loved by a good-looking man who can have his pick of women. And you *are*, Harper. You're the most worthy person I know."

Em was glaring at her now. God, she even looked cute when she was angry. "Stop hiding your light under a bushel."

Harper blinked. A bushel? Apparently she was cute and *biblical* when angry.

"And don't let Dex hide your light, either. You need to go to that gala without him and flaunt that ass and every single curve right in his face. Let him see you're just fine without him. Let him know what he's missing out on. Hell, I'm going to come with you just to make sure you do it right."

"You are?"

"Fucking A," Em confirmed.

"It sounds kinda high school, don't you think?" Even though Harper had done the same thing that day she'd dropped her gown on him. But at least it had been in private, with no chance of public humiliation if it backfired.

"There are times to be adult and times to make douchebags pay." Em clinked her shot glass against Harper's. "Now, drink up, you have a dress to try on."

Chapter Thirteen

Linc whistled under his breath as he and Dex waited for the other Smoke players to walk the red carpet. "Well *hellooo*, mumma." He nudged Dex. "Isn't that Harper Nugent? No wonder you've been fumbling the ball."

Dex turned, following Linc's gaze, and almost swallowed his tongue. It *was* Harper. She was in a stunning red dress that hugged her figure like a glove. It also featured a diamond cutout over her chest, exposing most of a bra that consisted of a red satin half-cup and red satin ribboning that followed the rounded proportions of her upper breasts. To cap it off, there was a tantalising strip of ribbon running horizontally across the bared swells of her cleavage at about nipple level, dividing the exposed flesh into fascinating segments.

Her dark brown hair shone under the lights and swung loose and wavy over her shoulders and down her back. She was tall and curvy and stunning — Xena, red-carpet princess — and Dex stared unblinking for long moments.

Hell, every male with a pulse stared.

He wanted to kill them all.

"You're a lucky man." Ryder, in a tux and his best black Akubra—in deference to the formality of the evening—clapped Dex on the back.

"Who's the cutie she's with?" Linc asked.

Dex shook himself out of his stunned inertia at the question. "That's her friend, Em."

Linc rubbed his hands together. "I bags Em," he announced, then grinned at his stupid pun.

"She's not a locker or the goddamn front seat," Dex said irritably. "She's a *person*." He stalked away, but not before he heard Bodie say, "I think he was happier when he wasn't getting laid."

He headed in Harper's direction, despite an internal warning light blinking madly, advising him to leave it the hell alone. He ignored it and ploughed on, although it was slow going, dodging people milling around on the carpet and those who had stopped to talk to media outlets stationed along the entrance. But he kept his eyes on the goal.

He and everyone else.

A soup of emotions he couldn't separate simmered in his gut. He'd assumed after what had transpired the last time they were together that Harper wasn't coming. God knew, he'd have gotten out of it if he'd been able. But here she was. Looking stunningly sexy.

"Harper," he said, when he finally managed to weave around the last excited group of gala goers. She had her back to him, and he absently noted how demure the dress was at this angle before he noted the stiffening of her shoulders.

She turned, her expression carefully neutral, her glossy mouth drawing his gaze. "Dexter," she said coolly, a small, taut smile stretching her mouth. Em had also turned, but her expression wasn't remotely neutral.

She was Team Harper all the way.

Now that he was here, he had no idea what to say to her.

Except maybe offering her his jacket. And wrapping her up in it. "I didn't think you'd be here after we…"

She smiled cynically. "Surprise."

His gaze dropped to her cleavage. How could it not? He clenched his hands at his side as the overwhelming urge to bury his face in those curves took hold. To yank her into the nearest private alcove and do her against the wall. "You look…"

His brain flicked through a host of possibilities. Hot. Sexy. Fuckable. He discarded them all. He didn't want to be lecherous.

Which left him with lame…"Nice," he said finally.

She stiffened further and Dex wished he could kick his own ass. He opened his mouth to try again but Em didn't give him the chance.

"Nice?" she hissed, her glare on full tilt. "Are you *fucking* kidding me?" she demanded, keeping her voice low. "Harper is so far out of the ballpark of nice, she's on another freaking planet. In case you haven't noticed, she has curves and cleavage most women would kill for. And seeing as how you've made it very clear that *balls* and not *boobs* are your thing, she's going to have a good time flaunting them around here tonight, and I'd appreciate it if you'd stay the hell away from her."

Finished with her diatribe, she grabbed a solemn looking Harper by the arm. "Come on, girlfriend. Let's go show those puppies off to guys who actually appreciate them."

And then they were both gone.

• • •

Suffice to say, Dex *did not* enjoy the night. Being in the same ballroom as Harper was bad enough. Being in the same ballroom as Harper in *that dress* was a frickin' nightmare. He watched every man in the room stop by her table, ostensibly to *congratulate* her on the murals that were being projected onto all the walls, but really to have a conversation with her cleavage.

Which she seemed to be *lapping* up.

Anger and frustration simmered in his blood. And something else that felt too big, too intense, too...terrible to identify. Something that was making him crazier and crazier. So crazy he barely noticed any of his surroundings. Not the beautifully decorated tables, not the people he knew, not the conversations going on around him.

"This is such a cool idea," Valerie said, admiring the pink, heart-shaped toy ring on her middle finger.

Each place had been set with a small goody bag, and amidst the things inside had been one of those plastic balls that popped out of vending machines loved by kids everywhere. The balls contained the usual junk—toy rings and necklaces and miniature plastic cars. The vending machine company was one of the event's sponsors.

Dex had no idea what was in his ball. He didn't even look at his goody bag. He just sat there, brooding, trying and failing not to look at Harper, his mood getting blacker and blacker. Tanner and Matilda sitting to one side of him, and Linc and Valerie on the other, had given up trying to get any civilised conversation out of him.

How he got through the meal, he didn't know. Then the dancing started and he had to watch Harper *dancing* with what felt like every guy in the room. His table companions came and went to the dance floor, but Dex just sat and brooded.

Women dropped by and asked him to dance, to which he politely declined, citing a training injury, until Tanner finally said, "Enough, Dex. Dance with someone or go home. Your fake injury is going to reach the media tables soon, and Griff will be even more pissed off at you than he is at the moment."

Linc chose that moment to come back to table. "Okay," he announced, rubbing his hands. "I'm going to ask Em to dance."

"I wouldn't if I were you," Dex said morosely. "She's knocked back every guy who's asked so far. She broke up with someone not long ago, and if that evil glare is anything to go by, she's still not very male friendly."

"I hate to tell you, buddy"—Linc slapped him on the back—"but that evil glare is solely for *you*. I, on the other hand, am charming and hot and have just the right kind of rebound sex a woman like Em needs. I'll risk it."

"Wait." Dex stood as Linc turned to go. "I'll be your wing man."

And damn it all—if Harper could dance with every other guy at the gala she could damn well dance with him.

Valerie glanced at Tanner as they departed. "I think you'd better go with them. He looks like he's going to punch the next guy who comes within a metre radius of Harper."

"Yes." Matilda nodded her agreement. "What the hell is wrong with him? I've never seen him so…cranky. He's usually so contained."

"He's in love," Tanner stated, with an assurance that had captained the Smoke to three premierships in a row. "He just doesn't know it yet."

"I sure as hell hope you're going to be the one to tell him," Matilda said, looking at Tanner expectantly.

"I was hoping he'd figure it out by himself."

"And how's that worked out?" she asked, her smile sweet, her gaze unrelenting.

"Not so good," Tanner admitted, looking like he'd rather be bringing Dex news about his latest STD status. "Guess he needs to hear it straight."

Matilda smiled and patted him on the arm. "My hero."

By the time they reached Harper, Dex had built up a full head of steam. She was back at the table, in between dancing partners, and he had to grip his hands around the empty chair next to her to stop himself from reaching for her.

"Hey," Linc said, smiling down at Em like she was something particularly delicious he wanted to spread on toast. Possibly even his sheets, if she was amenable. "I understand you're in the market for some rebound sex, and I reckon I'm your guy. I have no morals, amazing ball control, and stamina to burn. Fancy a dance?"

Em looked at Linc like he was something particularly nasty on the bottom of her shoe. She shot him a twisted smile capable of shrinking testicles in a three table radius. "I would rather drink poison."

Linc shot Em his winning smile. Dex had seen it enough times to know it had a reasonably high success rate. "I'll be your poison, baby, just name it."

A guy with one of those trendy bushranger beards and *no clue* approached the table, smiling at Harper and asking her to dance. His hand rested on her shoulder, and Dex just about burst a blood vessel in his brain.

"Dude," he said, fixing his gaze on Harper's shoulder. "You better take your hand off her, or I'm going to break your fingers."

The guy, clearly recognising Dexter immediately, threw up his hands and apologised, stepping slowly away. "Sorry, man, I didn't realise she was your girlfriend."

Harper glared at Dex as the guy backed away and disappeared into the general hubbub of the crowd, but he was over any kind of rationality. "Dance with me," he said, his heart beating so loud in his ears he could barely hear the music pumping out from the band.

Hell, he could barely contain himself from hauling her up and dragging her onto the dance floor.

"No." She glanced at Linc who was clearly looking for another inroad with the aloof Em. "But I'll dance with you," she said, smiling at him.

Linc, attuned to any woman's interest no matter how facile, switched his attention to Harper's cleavage. "Delighted." He grinned.

Dex's blood pressure spiked into the danger zone. He looked at his teammate and friend. "Touch her, and I'll break *your* fingers, too."

Harper, clearly dissatisfied with his macho crap glared at him. "You gonna break the fingers of every guy here tonight?"

Dex nodded. "If I have to."

Harper shook her head at him. "What the hell is your problem?" she snapped.

A film of red washed over Dex's vision. "Did you have to wear something so revealing?" he demanded.

She blinked. "Why not? The WAGS are wearing stuff just as revealing as I am."

Dex didn't give a shit what Matilda and the other wives and girlfriends were revealing. He cared what *she* was putting out there.

He cared a lot.

Not because she was flaunting it, but because she was flaunting to everyone but him. The thought made him want to whip off his jacket. "The WAGS aren't you."

Her eyes hardened at his growly response, and he realised too late that she'd misconstrued his words. He hadn't meant she couldn't compare. He'd meant he didn't give a flying fuck what *they* wore or didn't.

But for someone as sensitive about her appearance as Harper, it had been a stupid thing to say.

Unfortunately, she didn't give him a chance to correct

himself. "*Don't*," she hissed, rising to her feet, her temper obviously frayed to the point of snapping. "Don't you *dar*e come over here when you don't want me, telling everyone else they can't have me, either. *Don't* be ashamed of being seen with me in public then stop others who aren't."

Dex noted the heavy drag of her breath as those fascinating ribbons moved up and down in front of his eyes.

"*Oookay,* big guy." A hand as heavy as an All Black forward row landed on his shoulder. *Tanner.* "Let's go get some air, huh?"

The Smoke skipper smiled apologetically at Harper before glancing at Linc in an encompassing *that means you, too,* glare. Dex wanted air about as much as he wanted a kick in the balls. But Harper was furious, Em looked like she wanted to smash a plate over his head, and they were obviously attracting a bit of a crowd.

Dex drew in a shaky breath as Tanner pulled on his arm. Somehow he'd made things worse, and he had no desire to be on the front page of the papers tomorrow morning for being a dick. Even if he *was* being a dick. He left reluctantly with Tanner and Linc, but it didn't stop him from wanting to beat his chest in absolute frustration.

"I got this," Tanner said to Linc, keeping firm hold of Dex's arm.

Linc nodded and headed back to their table as Dex let himself be led to the exit. "You going to tell me what's up with you?" Tanner said once he'd dragged Dex far enough away from the noise of the ballroom and the stares of curious onlookers. "Or do you want me to guess?"

Dex slumped against the wall. "Harper."

Tanner snorted. "*Harper* is not what's up with you. *You* are what's up with you."

"Gee, thanks, man." Dex glared at his so-called friend. "Your support is overwhelming."

"Okay, fine." Tanner held up his hands in a surrender gesture. "Tell me, then."

Dex wished he knew where to start. He shoved a hand through his hair. "I don't know what's happening to me. She's driving me crazy."

Tanner nodded calmly as if the news was no surprise to him. "Because?"

Dex frowned. *Because?* What the fuck did he mean? "I don't know why. She's the first woman I've felt like I can be *me* around. I don't have to be *on* or pretend I'm somebody I'm not. She gets who I really am, beyond what the club and the media try to project. She actually couldn't care less about my rugby cred."

He glanced at Tanner for feedback, but he just stood there expectantly as if he was waiting for something.

"She says she loves me then she tells me she's not going to be my dirty little secret anymore. What the fuck?" he demanded of Tanner. "She's not that. She's *never* been that. I just don't want to share her with anyone yet, but she thinks that means I'm trying to hide her. I *hate* that she thinks that."

Another calm nod from Tanner. "Because?"

The blood vessel from earlier pulsed painfully at Dex's temple. His heart beat loud in his ears as pressure built in Dex's chest. "Because it's not *goddamn* true," he snapped. "Jesus. I can't eat or drink or sleep, she's got me tied in so many knots. Fuck, man, my whole game is off."

"Because?"

The pressure built some more at Tanner's insistent, annoying refrain. What did he want Dex to say? "Because…I think this thing with Harper is bigger than rugby. And frankly it scares the bejesus out of me."

Tanner smiled this time, like they'd just had some kind of breakthrough. "*Because?*"

Dex's blood pressure shot into stroke range as he

contemplated popping Tanner right in the kisser. "God-*fucking*- dammit." He glared at his best mate as the pressure inside his chest spiked then blew out in an almighty rush. "Because I love her, okay?"

There was a moment of stunned silence from Dex, the truth so startling that his mouth shut with an audible snap.

Tanner patted him on the shoulder. "Atta boy." He grinned. "Wasn't so hard, was it?"

The revelation sunk in like a lead balloon, unable to be ignored or denied anymore. *Christ.* What a fucking blind fool he'd been. It was so *obvious* now. He wasn't the same guy he'd been before he'd dared Harper Nugent to a game of strip Battlefront and ended up doing the wild thing on her couch.

No matter how much he'd tried to tell himself nothing had changed.

Oh, he was still *him,* but he was aware of the differences now. Like all his cells had been reprogrammed and there was something inherently *changed* about him. He just hadn't realised it until Tanner had forced him to dig deep.

He'd been too tunnel-visioned to allow anything outside of his career into the equation.

Dex shut his eyes and pinched the bridge of his nose. "This isn't the way I planned things."

Tanner laughed, and he opened his eyes. "Give it up, dude. This'll be better, trust me."

"I've got five years. I'm supposed to be concentrating on my football."

"And that's what you've been doing? Fumbling the ball? Fucking up line outs? That's you concentrating? Don't you think you'll be able to concentrate *better* when she's in your life for good? Because I gotta tell you, keeping her on the outside is *not* working for you."

Dex knew the truth of it. And it wasn't just about his rugby. Keeping Harper on the outside wasn't working for him in *any* way. He was leading a half-life. He might as well be back in Perry Hill. What was a career if he didn't have someone special to share it with?

"I don't want to do it without her anymore."

And with that, he surrendered every reservation, every mantra he'd ever lived by, and a huge weight lifted from his shoulders.

He felt free—and in love.

"Why are you telling me this?" Tanner grinned. "Go tell her."

Dex smiled back. He just wasn't sure he hadn't blown it completely. "She thinks I think she's not glamorous enough to be a WAG."

Tanner shrugged. "So go prove she is."

• • •

Harper's legs shook as she walked up the four stairs to the stage, both from nerves and from her last confrontation with Dex. If it hadn't been for this commitment, she'd have already left. Hell, if it had been up to her, Harper would have left after the red carpet incident, despite the obligation.

Not that Em would have allowed it.

The room was silent, and Harper felt acutely self-conscious, like every eye on her was judging her for what she was wearing and thinking how a woman her size should have chosen something a little more circumspect.

Why, oh why, had she worn something so revealing? Why had she listened to Em?

A few hours ago she'd felt proud and confident in the dress. It sure as hell had attracted a lot of attention. Dex's eyes had almost fallen out of his head for starters, and then she'd been hit on all night by a bunch of good-looking *single* guys.

It had been just what her ego had needed.

She'd spent so many years thinking of herself as unattractive because of her curviness, but she could see with her own two eyes tonight that men *did* find her attractive. That she could actually turn heads. Dex included.

Em had been right about Harper's feelings of unworthiness, but tonight had started to redress that. Until Dex had opened his mouth. And now the doubt demons were back.

The WAGS aren't you.

In one sentence, Dex has squashed her confidence.

The emcee, Dan, a hot young paediatric doc from the hospital introduced her and the audience clapped. A guy at the front table, who Harper could just make out under the rim of the stage lights, half stood, put his thumb and forefinger in his mouth, and let a loud wolf whistle rip. He smiled at her, clutching his chest dramatically and tapping his fingers to mimic his beating heart as he sat down. Everyone at the nearby tables laughed and cheered, and it was a good boost to her flagging ego.

Harper stood a little taller.

Dan boosted it some more by bowing with a low flourish at the end of his spiel then playfully kissed her hand. He had flirty eyes and Harper noticed the same interest she'd seen in a lot of men tonight.

She smiled as she took her place at the podium, and the audience hushed. She didn't know if Dex was out there in the darkness beyond the glare of the lights. She'd watched Tanner hustle him outside earlier, and she had no idea if they'd returned. She tried not to think about it. This moment wasn't about him.

It was her moment.

The mural projections had gone down a treat, and Harper could talk about her art all night. And who knew where this type of exposure could lead?

She launched into her speech about her creative process, as requested by the hospital executive, putting Dex firmly out of her mind. The audience was engrossed in it, and in the images she'd put together into a presentation. When she was done, Dan, along with some helpers carrying spare mics on the floor, facilitated a Q & A session.

Harper was thrilled with how well it appeared to be going. People seemed genuinely interested in her and the murals. It didn't stop the now-certain feeling that Dex was somewhere beyond the blaze of lights watching her—her skin prickled with it. But if anything, his presence made her more gregarious in her answers.

She had this crowd in the palm of her hand—she could feel it—and she was going to work it whether he approved or not.

"I think we have time for a couple of more questions," Dr Dan said in a voice Harper was sure soothed a lot of frazzled mothers.

"Yes." The guy who'd wolf-whistled stood, and Harper smiled at him as he was handed the mic. "I'd like to know are you single, and would you come out on a date with me?"

Harper blinked at the unexpected question as the audience laughed. "Oh." She blushed and couldn't help but laugh also.

"Yeah," another guy said, somewhere at the back, "Me, too."

"And me."

Harper's cheeks warmed as two more guys stood and asked for a date as the crowd clapped and cheered each one.

"Looks like you have some admirers, Harper," Dan grinned. "Guess you'd better put them out of their misery. *Are* you single?"

Harper tossed her head and stared in the direction of Dex's table even if she couldn't see it properly. "Yes."

There were cheers from the crowd. "Well, now," Dan said, obviously good at ad-libbing and taking the pulse of the crowd. "This wasn't exactly what we'd planned, but maybe we should earn some money for the hospital out of this. What do you reckon, Harper? Shall we have an impromptu auction? A date with you to the highest bidder? All proceeds going to the hospital? What'd you say?"

Harper nodded and laughed. Why the hell not? It was a good cause after all. And the fact that Dex was here to witness it? Win/win.

Dan looked out over the ballroom. "Who's prepared to put their money where their mouth is? And remember…" He put his hand across his heart to really work the pathos. "It's for the sick kiddies."

"One thousand," the guy at the front offered with a grin.

"Two," came from the back but it was impossible for Harper to see because of the lights.

From somewhere over to the left: "Three."

And somewhere near that: "Four."

"Eight," the cocky guy at the front threw in, to a few *ooohs* from the rapt crowd.

"One hundred thousand dollars."

The granite voice needed no microphone to carry. And even across an entire ballroom it had the ability to tighten her nipples. A collective gasp rang around the room as heads swivelled in search of who had made the outrageous bid. Harper didn't have to search—she *knew,* and her breath momentarily stuttered to a halt.

What the hell…? For the love of all that was holy, the stupid man could have dated her for *free*.

"But I want more," he said.

There was gravel in his voice now, and if there was a woman in the room not thinking of Dex naked on his knees, begging for more, Harper would like to meet her.

There was a stir amongst the audience, passing from one table to the next as heads turned toward the stage. He was on the move.

Harper couldn't be sure, because she couldn't really see, but she could sense him getting closer. She felt it in her gut.

And places slightly lower.

"Hey," the guy at the front protested good-naturedly as Dex appeared at the stage, taking the steps two at a time. "What's he got that I don't?"

"He's got balls," someone yelled from the side.

"Yeah, and he rucks like a demon," someone else joked, and everyone laughed.

Before she knew it, his tuxedoed form was on the stage and heading for her. Harper's pulse accelerated. She could tell herself—*she could tell the whole damn room*—she was single, but she was always going to belong to this man.

Heat flushed Harper's cheeks as a pregnant silence fell over the audience. What the fuck was he doing? Was he drunk and having a Kanye moment? "Dex?" She glanced at the rapt crowd and back at him. "What are you doing?" she whispered, but with the microphone right there, it wasn't exactly private.

He slid his hands up her arms and turned her slightly to face him. "I'm apologising for being, in the words of Hugh Grant, 'a daft prick,' and I'm begging your forgiveness." Someone in the crowd let out an almighty wolf whistle, and there were sporadic claps and cheers. "I can't eat or drink or sleep for thinking about you. I sure as shit can't play rugby."

"You got that right," someone in the audience called out, and everyone laughed.

"But I don't care about that." Dex slogged on, his fingers warm and firm around her biceps. "I don't care if I don't play another game of rugby ever again, because you mean more to me than it *ever* has. And if you want me to give it up, I will do it in a heartbeat. I'll give up everything. Hell, I'd even go back to Perry Hill, as long as you come with me. I don't care if we have to live on mac and cheese for the rest of our lives if it means you're by my side, because I love you, Harper Nugent."

More wolf whistling and clapping echoed around the ballroom. "I am madly, stupidly, desperately in love with you. I just didn't want to see it."

He paused for a breath, then, and the audience clapped and hollered some more. Harper's heart was beating so fast in her chest she didn't know how it was actually pumping effectively. Hot tears pricked the back of her eyes as she searched his calm green gaze for signs of disingenuousness.

There wasn't any.

She couldn't believe this was happening to her. *He loved her?* She'd dreamed about him saying those three little words but hadn't believed she'd ever hear them. She certainly never thought he'd declare himself in front of a ballroom full of mostly strangers and a shitload of media.

And he wasn't finished yet.

"In front of the four hundred people here tonight," he continued, "and the hundreds and thousands of people who will see this on their television and the millions more who will see it the second someone here uploads the video they're taking right now to Facebook"—more audience laughter—"I want you to know how sexy you are. How much I love your curves, how *obsessed* I am with your ass"—clapping and wolf whistling interrupted him and he waited for it to die down—"and how seeing you in your baggy painting overalls, the ones with the zip that goes all the way down the front, makes me want to do *real* bad things to you."

Harper blushed furiously as the audience erupted, her pulse tripping. The entire ballroom filled with the sound of stamping feet. She'd accused Dex of keeping her as a dirty little secret, of being embarrassed by her body.

Well, he'd just blown that complaint right out of the water.

She knew what an intensely private man Dex was and how hard this must be for him, to bare his soul in front of everyone. But he was giving it his all.

His hands slid down her arms to clasp her hands that were trembling like crazy.

"But more than that, I love how you kick my ass in Battlefront, I love how you are with Jace and Tabby, I love your sense of humour and I am in awe of your artistic talent and how you volunteer your time to teach art to the kids at the hospital. And more than anything, I love how being with you feels like coming home and I don't want to live another day without you in my life. "

He dropped down on one knee. Harper's eyes widened as her stomach went into free fall.

"What are you doing, Dex?" she whispered as the crowd went wild.

But he just squeezed her hands and smiled at her. "Harper Nugent," he said when the noise died down. In fact the whole ballroom fell silent as if holding its breath. "I know we haven't known each other for very long, but I love you. I want us to be together forever. Would you do the honour of marrying me?"

Everyone in the room sprang to their feet, clapping like crazy. Harper stood, stunned, looking down into his breathtakingly handsome face as the crowd hushed again, waiting for her answer.

Could this *really* be happening?

"I'm sorry, I don't have a ring for you right now," he said. "I hadn't really planned this."

Harper gave a half-laugh. *Clearly*. He was obviously suffering from temporary insanity. Or maybe it was a sign they should slow things down. She didn't want any buyer remorse come tomorrow. "Maybe you need to think about it a bit more?"

He shook his head. "Hell no, baby. When I know what I

want I go for it, and I want you. Every day. Not just Sundays. And I'm not going to rest until I put a ring on it."

"Hey, Dex!" The interruption brought Harper back to the reality of where they were. Suddenly Tanner was jogging up to the stage. When he was close enough, he lobbed something which Dex, still on bended knee, duly caught. It was the round plastic ball from their goody bag, and he smiled at it as he cracked it open and a plastic ring with a gaudy red fake stone in the shape of a heart fell out into his hand.

"Well?" he said, holding it up. "What do you say?"

"Say yes," someone called out.

Harper smiled even as tears pricked her eyes, her chest so full of love for him she could barely breathe. He loved her and wanted to marry her. He thought she was sexy and proved it by his very public declaration.

What more could a woman ask for? Especially when she loved him so much it hurt.

"Yes," she whispered.

The audience went into meltdown as Dex shoved the ring on her finger then hauled himself to his feet. "But you can't give up rugby," she said, raising her voice over the mad applause as she planted a hand on his chest keeping him back. His pecs strained against her hold. "Because you've worked too hard for that. Plus, mac and cheese is not thigh friendly."

He grinned. "I, on the other hand, am *very* thigh friendly." He pulled her toward him and she went willingly. "Something I plan to prove to you every day."

Harper slid her arms around his neck, accepting the hungry slant of his mouth with an answering hunger of her own. It had only been a handful of days since he'd kissed her but it felt like an age.

And it was good. *Very* good. It felt like forever.

And promised it, too.

Epilogue

Harper couldn't believe the difference a month could make, as she and Dex hosted a BBQ in his back yard for the team and their families after their win the previous night.

She'd already moved in, turning Dex's sparsely appointed inner city pad into a home, instead of just a place to eat and sleep. Her furniture fit right in with the polished blonde floorboards, as did the addition of colourful rugs and curtains. Her art decorated the walls, and she'd just started working on a mural—a wicked version of the smoke and flames she'd painted on Dex's body—on the wall above their bed.

It was strong and masculine and turned her on just looking at it.

"So you guys set a date yet?" Valerie asked, as a few of them huddled around the BBQ watching Dex flip steaks and turn sausages. Jace and Tabby were frolicking in the nearby pool with some of the other kids, and the smell of charred beef and frying onions hung heavy in the air.

"As soon as humanly possible," Dex growled, slipping an arm around Harper's waist and planting a kiss on her neck.

"Dude," Linc said. "Don't tell me you've put a bun in her oven already? Jeez!"

Donovan clipped Linc across the head. "Just because no one wants to be impregnated with your demon spawn doesn't mean others don't want to procreate."

Linc grinned, completely unabashed. He winked at Em, who was standing next to Harper. "Yeah, but plenty of women want my demon *seed*."

Em folded her arms. "Not even in the ninth circle of hell. Not even if you were the last man on earth."

Linc clutched at his heart as if he'd been wounded, and everyone laughed. Harper had to give it to Em. She'd stuck to her guns where men were concerned, and Harper was damn proud of her. Em was working her shit out, and she was stronger because of it.

"No," Dex said, looking into her eyes as the laughter died down, and Harper's heart just about burst out of her chest. "We're not pregnant. But I can't wait to give this woman one more curve."

He kissed her then, and she melted into him, uncaring of their audience. It was hard to believe this man who had wanted only rugby a couple of months ago now wanted it all. Rugby, marriage, kids.

The whole enchilada.

"Yeah, yeah," Ryder grouched. "You're going to incinerate the bloody snags if you're not careful."

Harper pulled away, grinning. "I want a whole damn rugby team, Dexter Blake."

There was clapping and cheering at her statement, and Harper's chest felt tight. She was a part of them, and she was so grateful to these guys and their women for the way they'd embraced her.

Dex's eyes widened a little bit, then he broke into a grin, too. "You're on. Is it rude to ask everybody to leave so we can get started?"

Harper laughed. "It's okay, we've got time." And she kissed him again.

They had all the time in the world.

Glossary

I've probably used some words in here that some readers may not know—both rugby ones and strange Aussie-isms alike. So I thought a handy-dandy glossary might help. It is, of course, written entirely from my perspective and so is heavily biased, female-centric, and quite possibly dodgy. It probably wouldn't stand up to any kind of official scrutiny.

Footy—We love this term in Australia. The confusing thing for most non-Aussies is they never know which game it refers to because we have three separate but distinct codes of football in Australia:

1. Rugby League (Jarryd Hayne played this code before he went and played Gridiron).

2. Rugby union—the code the Sydney Smoke play, and the one this series is based upon (Jarryd Hayne tried his hand at this code for a bit after the whole Gridiron thing didn't work out but is now back playing League).

3. Aussie rules football—different altogether. Tall, fit guys in really tight shorts.

There is also soccer but we don't really think of that as football in the traditional sense here in Australia.

The confusing thing is we refer to all of them as the footy, e.g., "Wanna go to the footy, Davo?" And somehow we all seem to know which code is being referred to at any given time. Even more confusing, the ball that is used in each code is often also called the footy, e.g., "Chuck me the footy, Gazza."

Pitch—Apparently the rugby field is called a pitch but colloquially here we just call it the footy (see, I told you we liked that term) field. A pitch is more a cricket term. No, don't worry, I won't ever try to explain to you a game that lasts five days...

Ruck—No, not a typo. That's ruck with an R, ladies! Happens after a tackle as each team tries to gain possession of the ball.

Line-out—that weird thing they use to restart play where each team lines up side by side, vertical to the sideline, and one of the guys throws the ball to his team and a few of the guys from that team bodily lift one dude up to snatch the ball out of the air. It's like rugby ballet. Minus the tutus. And usually with more blood.

Scrum—another way to gain possession of the ball. I'm going to paraphrase several definitions I've read: a scrum is when two groups of opposing players pack loosely together, arms interlocked, heads down, jockeying for the ball that is fed into the scrum along the ground. It's like a tug of war with no rope and more body contact or, as I like to call it, a great big man hug with a lot of dudes lying on top of each other at the end of it all. Very homoerotic. Win/win.

Try—a goal. Except in rugby union, we don't say someone scored a goal, we say someone scored a try after they've dived for the line and a bunch of other guys have jumped on top to try and stop it from happening. Very homoerotic. Win/win. A try is worth five points.

Haka—a ceremonial dance performed by all Polynesian cultures but made famous by the New Zealand All Blacks rugby team, who perform it before every match in an awesome, spine-chilling display of power, passion, and identity. I'm sure it's only coincidental that it's also crap-your-pants scary. There are few things more fearsome than an advancing All Black haka!

WAGS—wives and girlfriends. These are partners of the dudes that play rugby. Although we also use the term here in Oz to refer to partners of our cricket players. I think in the UK, WAGS is also a term used for football (soccer) partners.

Pash—not a footy term but one I used a couple of times that confused the heck out of my editor. A pash is a kiss e.g. "Did you pash him, Shazza." It's the Aussie equivalent to the British term snog.

Akubra—an iconic Australian brand of hat worn by country guys and gals. Vaguely similar to the Stetson, but I'll probably have my nationality revoked for saying so! It has a distinctive shape that's about as Aussie as vegemite.

Chocolate topping—this is what we call chocolate syrup and you put it on your ice cream. Although I'm fairly sure it gets put on other things as well, none of them food.

Lolly—Americans call it candy, the Brits call it a sweetie, we call 'em lollies.

Arvo—in that long tradition of shortening everything and sticking an O on the end, this is Aussie for afternoon, e.g., "Hey Robbo, whatcha doin' this arvo?"

Wank—to wank is to masturbate. Pretty much always referring to a guy. Although, we embrace all terms for this biological process. Jerking/jacking/tossing off are well known, as is spanking the monkey and choking the chicken (or chook, as we say here). There's also the term "wanker," which is actually rarely used to describe one who wanks. We much prefer to use this as an insult for someone who is a bit of a jerk, e.g., "That Johnno is a wanker."

Acknowledgments

My thanks, as always, go to the team at Brazen. A hell of a lot of work goes on behind the scenes to get these fabulous books into your hands, and it's much appreciated. Special thanks to Kaitlyn Osborn for doing all that publicity stuff, and to Liz Pelletier for her editing insights, her collaboration, and her cheerleading.

To Heather Howland for the fabulous cover, and Lindee Robinson, photographer, for shooting it. A cover shoot has long been on my author bucket list, and I am beyond thrilled that this has finally come to fruition.

My undying gratitude to David Grice and Jon O'Brien for their continued help with all the rugby stuff I don't understand. There's Google, but these guys are better.

About the Author

Multi-award-winning and *USA Today* bestselling author Amy Andrews is an Aussie who has written fifty romances, from novellas to category to single-title in both the traditional and digital markets for a variety of publishers. Her first love is steamy contemporary romance that makes her readers tingle, laugh, and sigh. At the age of sixteen, she met a guy she instantly knew she was going to marry, so she just smiles when people tell her insta-love books are unrealistic because she did marry that man and, twenty-odd years later, they're still living out their happily ever after.

She loves good books, fab food, great wine, and frequent travel—preferably all four together. She lives on acreage on the outskirts of Brisbane with a gorgeous mountain view but secretly wishes it were the hillsides of Tuscany.

Discover the **Sydney Smoke Rugby** *series…*

Also by Amy Andrews

SCORING THE PLAYER'S BABY
a *WAGS* novel by Naima Simone

After divorcing her cheating football player ex, Kim Matlock would rather cut out her own heart than work at a wedding expo. The last thing she expects is to be kissed breathless by a hot giant looking to fend off a stalker. She doesn't want relationships, but she agrees to one scorching night with the sexy stranger. To her shock, she finds out afterward that a) he's a pro football player, and b) she's pregnant.

HITTING IT
a *Locker Room Diaries* novel by Kathy Lyons

If journalist Heidi Wong wants to keep her job, she needs to come up with a story—fast! That's why she tells her boss that she knows the Bobcat's reclusive new slugger, Rob Lee. And she does...in the Biblical sense. But everyone knows reporters and athletes don't mix. Or do they?

ENGAGING THE BACHELOR
a *Pulse* novel by Cathryn Fox

Hot, Southampton doctor, Carson Reynolds isn't the kind of man Gemma Carr should be playing with. But his offer of a fake engagement comes with sexy, late night house calls, and despite her bad girl reputation, it's been far too long since she's taken two and called anyone in the morning. But is she asking for a prescription for trouble?

WORKED UP
a *Made in Jersey* novel by Tessa Bailey

Factory mechanic Duke Crawford just wants to watch SportsCenter in peace. Unfortunately, living with four divorcee sisters doesn't provide much silence, nor does it change his stance on relationships. But when fellow commitment-phobe Samantha Waverly stumbles into his life, he can't deny his protective instincts. The only way out of her family dilemma is to marry Duke—for show, of course. The blistering attraction between them might be hot enough to burn down the world, but their marriage isn't real...or is it?

Made in United States
Troutdale, OR
06/04/2024

20313352R00137